Richardson, Mozelle.
The song of India.   New York, Morrow, 1975.

208 p.   22 cm.

I. Title.   m

74

The
Song
of
India

By Mozelle Richardson

The Song of India

by
Mozelle Richardson

WILLIAM MORROW & COMPANY, INC.
NEW YORK 1975

Printed in the United States of America.

1 2 3 4 5   79 78 77 76 75

Book design: Helen Roberts

Library of Congress Cataloging in Publication Data

Richardson, Mozelle.
  The song of India.

  I. Title.
PZ4.R524So [PS3568.I319]   813'.5'4   74-17136
ISBN 0-688-00336-2

Dedicated to those others who made
the Passage to India with me

—especially Dub

For the pleasures of touch
Have a beginning and end
And lead only to sorrow.

—*The Bhagavad-Gita* 5.22

chapter I

A rugged October wind gusted from the north pushing small whitecaps across University Lake until they broke in raspy slush sounds at my feet. It tangled my hair and struck tears from my eyes and chilled my nose. It whistled with a stubborn intensity through the leaves that still clung to the blackjack oaks, and I kicked absently at loose pebbles that lined the shore, venting my frustration the only way I could. A wisp of hair stung my eyelids and I brushed it away impatiently. My face felt grim and permanently set in a strained mask. I jammed my hands deep into my pockets and took a double lung-filling breath of air and expelled it with one word. "Damn!"

The maddening thing about the whole affair was that I was being used. And for a good cause? Well, yes, if university endowments are that important—and I knew they were. But I was being used—exploited is the better word—against my will. Compelled, pressured, coerced. It all boiled down to one thing. As long as your paycheck comes from one source, you have no rights.

Lane Thomas was sending me to India just at a time when it was least convenient for me to go. My university classes were getting into their regular swing. I had three new commissions for restorations that were a flattering acknowledgment of my growing reputation in the art world. The Sheridan Collection was to be previewed the following week at the Sheridan mansion under my supervision. The invitations were out; it was the art event of the year—a real coup for Midwestern University to acquire the most complete collection of Indian and Oriental art in the United States. And now I wouldn't be there. I'd be in India carrying greetings from an old lady to her niece.

I kicked viciously at a stone and watched it roll down the embankment, dislodging others to splash in the water. I watched the widening ripples until they collided with the miniature waves and were lost. That's me, I thought. Trying desperately to make a ripple, and I come up against a gale and foolish whitecaps. The wind rustled those leaves that were left, stirring those that had fallen into quick whirlwinds that scattered them across the little peninsula where I stood, and settled them in pockets where blackened stones outlined bonfire sites, and sent others whirling into the lake where they were tossed about like runty boats in a storm.

I pulled my coat around me, walked up the embankment where the woods began, and sat down on a flat boulder braced against a moss-stained oak. The wind inched its way through my clothes, and I shivered. At least it would be warm in India. And I'd be going back to my favorite place in the world. I'd even been offered unlimited funds in case I found any antiquities the University Museum could use. There were three positive reasons why I should feel fortunate Miss Dameron picked me out of the department to go to India for her. But I didn't.

My shoulder bag hung rigid with its weight almost touching the ground. I reached in to pull out a sheathed dagger and laid it across my knees. An anemic sun filtered coolly through the trees and struck sparks from its jeweled hilt. It was the same Deccan *Katar* that the stranger had been examining when I walked into the museum gallery a week ago. I'd stopped when I saw him. He seemed so familiar that I started to speak. But when he glanced up and our eyes met there was no recognition in his. Only a curious look of anger that surprised me.

His glance bored through me as though I weren't there, then went back to examining the dagger. My greeting died in my throat. I knew we had never met; still, the feeling persisted. I passed by him into my office, but he didn't lift his eyes. I unlocked the door, then turned to look back. He was tall, hunched over the case with both arms resting on its slanted top, his head dipped forward so that a shock of hair fell over his forehead. It was thick, windblown, and so black that it took on a blue sheen under the skylight.

He wore scruffy jeans and a heavy sweater with leather patches at the elbows. No one could have looked more American. Yet somehow I knew he wasn't.

I closed the door and sat down at my desk, wondering what there was about him that made me so curious and what there was about the dagger—certainly the most beautiful item in the museum—that would make him so angry. I felt a vague sense of anxiety.

Late that afternoon when there was no one in the museum, I unlocked the case and removed the Deccan *Katar,* leaving a typed note in its place, *Item #701 removed for repairs,* and initialed it *BB.* It had been in my bag since. Now I eased it out of its jeweled velvet sheath. It rested heavy in my hand. I loved the feel of it—its weight

--•◦{ 3 }◦•--

was perfectly balanced, and I examined it again as I had a hundred times since I'd taken it from the museum.

It was mine. Corraway Sheridan—Uncle Coe—had given it to me when I graduated from the university and won the Sheridan Scholarship. He had been so proud—and I had, too. Then I loaned it to the University Museum when I went to India for the two years' study under the scholarship.

Certainly the dagger needed no repairs. It was as perfect now as when it had been crafted in the seventeenth century for an Indian prince. The hilt lay cool in the palm of my hand—a finely executed floral design in gold koftgari. A fiery chain of cabochon rubies circled the pommel which curved into a solid gold tiger's head with emerald eyes and ivory fangs. A fine gold cord and tassel, fastened with one perfect diamond, was knotted around his neck. It was an exquisite thing—a decorative weapon which had been the inspiration for my doctoral thesis on Indian swords. I'd used a color photograph of it for the frontispiece.

I ran my finger along the watered wootz blade, stiletto-sharp as the day it was honed, then slipped it back into its pale green velvet sheath with the age-darkened pearls, the rough-cut rubies, emeralds, sapphires, the gold tendrils which had been cleverly set into the case as a continuation of the trailing gold vines and jeweled flowers in the hilt. It was surely the most valuable thing I would ever own, and a splendid heritage from the India I knew so well.

Beyond the far reach of the lake, behind Academy Hill, the sun slipped into a whirl of clouds and turned them into a witches' cauldron of fermenting froth. It made the sky seem warmer than when the sun, pale and colorless, had sifted through the trees. Silhouetted darkly against the rose and saffron sky was the spire of Old Central, its gold-leaf face glowing with inflexible dignity. I fancied I heard its chimes. I should go; there was much to do.

But I made no effort to leave. Replacing the sheathed dagger carefully in my shoulder bag, I thought again of the man who had been so interested in it. I saw him shortly afterward at the faculty reception. Lane Thomas, dean of my department, brought him. It seemed that he was some dignitary from the Indian Embassy in Washington who was visiting art museums in the Midwest. I missed his name because I was so busy trying to think where I'd seen him before and wondering why he'd shown such anger as he looked at the *Katar*. His eyes were pale, almost the same color as his skin, a tawny gold-brown surprising to find in an Indian national. He was even taller than I remembered, standing almost head and shoulders above me.

I wondered if we'd met in India, then rejected the idea quickly. If I'd ever met the man before, I'd not have forgotten him. Not his strange Scorpio eyes that gave me a peculiar feeling of unease.

Instead of acknowledging our introduction with the customary "I'm delighted to meet you, Dr. Blakley," he said, his voice crisp with an Oxford accent, "Dr. Thomas tells me you own the Deccan *Katar*."

My smile faded. "That's right."

"I want to buy it."

I looked up at him quickly. "You're surely not serious!"

"But I am, Dr. Blakley."

"Then you must not realize its value. Of course it's not for sale." Before he could answer I turned and walked away. I felt him staring after me, and goose pimples pricked my back.

That night I dreamed I was flying over University Lake with great feathered wings holding the Deccan *Katar* close to my breast when a hunter came out of the trees. He turned his eyes on me and pierced my heart with a single dagger-point glance and I fell—dropping the *Katar*. I watched it splash into the lake, and as I followed, frantically trying to retrieve it before the hunter, I awoke. I was sitting up in bed, my heart pounding, clutching the sheet as though to keep from drowning. Then I heard a splash of water in the shower and laughed. I'd meant to get the spigot fixed. What peculiar influences a little noise can have on the subconscious! I turned over, ignored the continuing splashes, and went back to sleep.

The following morning Lane Thomas called me into his office. He seated me rather ceremoniously and I wondered if I was there for a reprimand or a raise. He leaned back in his swivel chair, rolled a pencil between his palms, and said, "Bevan, how would you like to go to India?"

The suddenness of his question caught me unaware. I looked at him suspiciously. There had to be a catch somewhere. The school year was just getting into full swing and there was no reason why I should go to India—now. I felt intuitively that it had something to do with the Indian and my Deccan *Katar*. I asked, "When?"

"As soon as you can get your visa."

"Well, of course, Lane, you know I'm taking a sabbatical next year and going. Right now it's out of the question. Classes are running smoothly, their routine is set, there are those three restoration jobs I'm scheduled to finish for the State Museum—and, of course, the Sheridan Collection and getting everything ready for the showing. It's simply impossible. But thanks anyway."

Lane looked at me over his glasses. "This is pretty important, Bevan. Your graduate assistant—Jacobs, isn't it?—can handle your classes until you return. The other things will have to wait."

The atmosphere was getting thick and I felt the hackles rise. "If I'm supposed to be curious, Lane, I am. Just remember—if I don't think I should go, I can refuse easily enough." I smiled sweetly, but he didn't return it. Instead his face was set stubbornly grim.

"You know Miss Edith Dameron." It wasn't a question; it was a statement of fact. There was no one in the state who didn't know her.

"Naturally," I answered, "who doesn't?" Edith Dameron had given several millions of her deceased father's oil fortune to the university. There was the freshman girls' dormitory called Edith Dameron; there was the Dameron Stadium, the athletic showplace of the Midwest; there was the Jason Dameron Health Center; and as much as I hated it, carved in marble over the entry of the University Museum in oversized Greek-style lettering were the two words, *Dameron Museum*. Even the four-faced clock on the Old Central spire had been repaired and gold-leafed with Dameron money. There was the Dameron Oak and the Dameron window over the altar in the chapel. There was the Dameron Dam which held back the waters of two streams to form University Lake—and we were prone to reverse and misspell the words.

The Damn Damerons damn near owned the university, and any given year I expected the regents to change the name from Midwestern U. to Jason Dameron U. I nodded grimly. I certainly did know Edith Dameron, a wizened little gray-haired witch with more money than blood.

Without changing expression Lane continued, "And you remember Elizabeth Dameron." Again it was a statement and not a question. He knew well enough that Miss

Edith's beautiful headstrong niece was not one of my favorite people. She'd been a student of mine for four years. I think—to consider it honestly—that it was because of the Dameron money I resented her. When she showed up at the university her freshman year with a ten-thousand-dollar sports car, wearing skintight jeans and a man's shirt hanging to her knees, with a face so beautiful it took your breath away, along with a full complement of friends and a genuine interest in Indian art and philosophy, I took an instant dislike to her.

In her four years at the University I was unable to fault her four-point record, although, frankly, I tried. If she was aware of my antagonism—and I couldn't believe she wasn't—she hid it very well. Many times she would seek me out in my office, on the campus, in the museum workshop, to talk about things Indian. The *Bhagavad-Gita,* the *Upanishads,* Hindu philosophy, dance, art, Sanskrit chants. Generally, when I found that I was enjoying the discussion too much, I'd find an excuse to break it off.

The year she graduated I voted against her receiving the Sheridan Scholarship. But mine was the only dissenting vote. She won the scholarship hands down.

I remembered when, in her junior year, she fell in love with the exchange professor from Cambridge. The entire faculty had been surprised when Dr. Gray's philosophy chair was filled by a brilliant young Hindu. We didn't know then that he was a maharaja's son.

"You knew she married Dr. Vehta?" Lane's question broke into my reverie.

"Yes. Although I never quite understood how," I added with the faintest tinge of sarcasm. "He returned to his home after that spring semester to marry the young princess he was betrothed to. Elizabeth talked to me about it. I didn't think it was wise to send her to India after that. . . ."

Lane looked at me with a half-smile that held no humor. "Was that why you were so against her getting the scholarship?"

I shrugged and looked past him out the window where the tops of the firs were black-green against the red and saffron of the oaks and maples, and the Old Central tower with its gold faces rose above them all in a slender spire that reminded me of the Deccan *Katar*. I had to pull my thoughts together to answer. "She was a student," I said, "and he was a professor. But more than that; their worlds were different—she could only get hurt."

I knew he didn't believe my concern for Elizabeth's welfare, but he didn't pursue it. "Well, Bevan, this might come as an unpleasant shock, but you've been delegated by Miss Edith to go to India to see Elizabeth."

"Me!" I started up from my chair and then settled back, looking at him through half-closed lids.

"You. Miss Dameron hasn't heard from Elizabeth in several months. There's no answer to her letters or cables. Yesterday she tried to call again and still couldn't get through to her. She's worried and wants you to go see her."

"That's the silliest thing I ever heard. Why doesn't she check through the American Embassy?"

"She has. They were informed through the Maharaja's representative that Elizabeth is fine."

"Then that should be that. Elizabeth obviously doesn't want the auntie messing up her life, and I can't say that I blame her. I'm not about to fly to India to say 'Hello' to a foolish girl just because she's teed off at Edith Dameron and her millions. Her Maharaja daddy-in-law could probably buy and sell Miss Edith several times over."

Lane's jaw stiffened; his eyes narrowed. "You're going to Kataipur, Bevan, whether you want to or not. It shouldn't take too long—a month or so."

"A month or so!"

He nodded, then added, slowly emphasizing each word, "If you decide you don't want to go, I'll accept your resignation right now."

I felt my face burn. "I can't believe I heard you say that." When he didn't answer I asked in a dry voice, "How much time do I have to think it over?"

"None."

I stood up and looked at him. "How can you do this to me—what have I ever done to you, Lane Thomas?"

He had the grace to lower his eyes. Pushing back his chair, he walked to the window. Finally he said, and I knew the words almost choked him, "You know the pressure is on me. What Miss Edith wants, Miss Edith gets."

"But why me?"

"Because you knew Elizabeth. Whether you liked her or not is beside the point. Because you speak Hindi—because you are the logical one to go see her."

I joined him at the window. "Why doesn't *she* go? Surely she'd like to see Elizabeth after three years—"

"She's concerned about Elizabeth, but doesn't want anyone there to think she's checking on her. She wants you to go as though you were on a buying trip for the university. That's why you need to stay at least a month. Bill Holmes will meet you there later. He's going to Nepal for Mr. Sheridan. It will be a business trip, and because you're in the neighborhood you'll drop in on Elizabeth as any old friend would—"

"Oh, brother! Sounds like a two-bit scenario. . . ."

He put his arm around my shoulder. "I know it does. But you'll go with an open expense account. Anything you find that you think the University Museum could use, buy it. The sky is the limit—now, don't you feel better?"

I shook my head. "Not particularly. It's infuriating—this—this power of money. And I'll resent it until the day I die."

"I know. I feel the same. But Miss Edith has done lots of good with hers, and the university has an insatiable appetite for money—"

"I feel rather like a character in a Greek drama—where the protagonist has no control over his destiny. So now I'm going to India. Hallelujah—bring on the chorus!"

"She also suggested you buy anything you want in the way of clothes."

"Ah," I answered nastily, "she is persuasive, isn't she?"

"Bitterness doesn't become you, Bevan—"

"Oh, I'm not bitter! It's simply that I've never been cast in the role of a puppet—and my strings are a little tangled." I turned on my heel and was at the door before Lane called, "Bevan, wait—"

I stopped, my hand on the doorknob, looking at him the way Jesus must have looked at Judas. "Mr. Pita-Singh —you met him at the reception—wants to buy your Deccan *Katar.*"

"Well?"

"He's prepared to pay an enormous amount of money for it—"

I shook my head slowly. "So everything is for sale! You can sell me, or even my department out from under me, but Lane, you can't sell my dagger—not ever—"

"Bevan, you don't understand. It's one of a pair that belonged to the Maharaja. Yours was stolen from them years ago. They want it back. And they're willing to pay—"

I walked back to his desk and leaned over it. "Lane Thomas, I'll tell you this. Nothing, absolutely nothing, will make me part with that dagger. Now I don't want to hear anything about it ever again. Do you understand?" I turned around and walked out of his office, slamming the door behind me. So the man with the strange eyes was still after my dagger. Walking to my office, I remembered the dream.

chapter II

Thinking about it now, I twisted uncomfortably on the rock. The clouds massed over Academy Hill had lost their color, leaving the sky a sullen gray. Across the lake, only a shade darker than the sky, misty points of light pricked where the campus worked its way around the bank. The red aircraft light on Old Central began its warning rounds —now you see it, now you don't. A galling irritation worked its way down my back and across my shoulders. It came from a mixture of feelings: the chill that inched through my coat; the tall Indian with the amber cat's eyes, who wanted my Deccan *Katar;* and, of course, the crux of it all—leaving at exactly the wrong time.

I stood up and looked at the night around me. University Lake had always been the haunt of lovers after dark—but that was during spring nights and summer evenings and in the autumn when the moon was full and the air fragrant with woodsmoke. Now there was no one except me to hear the slap of the water against the stones, the frozen call of a bird, the wind, lonesome through the trees.

When I was a little girl I'd come here with my grandfather and Uncle Coe. The three of us had walked its pebbled banks together many times. We fished and sailed and skimmed flat rocks across its surface. We had built bonfires on the barren peninsula to roast wieners and marshmallows. When I was older, it had become a refuge where I'd come to be by myself. It had comforted me when Grandfather died, it had shared my triumphs and my defeats, and it had fulfilled a need this evening. I brushed the dried bark and damp moss from my coat and walked back along the path, thick and soft with fallen leaves, to the road where I'd left the car.

Now I would go tell Uncle Coe good-bye—then I could leave tomorrow, my loose ends knotted neatly in place, with only a feeling of total frustration to remind me that this departure was a forced one.

It was Corraway Sheridan—Uncle Coe—who had molded my interests toward things Indian from the time I could walk. He and my grandfather had been great friends, and I remembered when I was a child curling up on the Isfahan rug in front of the fireplace listening to their talk of travel and world affairs—and always India. Uncle Coe had been there in the consular service, then afterward had returned often. It was his adopted country. His home, the old Sheridan mansion, was filled with treasures he'd brought back, and I never tired of listening to him tell about them. The Isfahan in front of the fireplace was a gift from the Nizam of Hyderabad after a favor. "What favor?" Grandfather had asked, and Uncle Coe, a handsome man with a ruddy complexion and thick sandy-gray hair, had winked. There was the full-breasted fifth-century terra-cotta maiden excavated from Asoka's palace at Pataliputra. "How'd you get that, Coe?" Grandfather had persisted. But Uncle Coe had smiled to himself and given a vague answer. There was the Czechoslovakian crystal library table that had been a gift from the Maharaja of Udaipur, and a sixteenth-century Tabriz rug from the Rani of Assam. "The Rani?" queried Grandfather. Uncle Coe had winked and smiled. "Charming woman," was all he said. Then there was the gold betel dish set with cabochon sapphires, a seventeenth-century Huqqa bowl inlaid with gold and silver, and the Emerald Kali. "God!" whispered my grandfather when he brought it out of its inlaid box. "Wherever did you get that? It's the most beautiful thing I ever saw!"

I scrambled under his arm to see it closer. I'll never forget the first look I had of it. Even then—I was no more than five years old—it took my breath, as it had each time I'd seen it since. Now, of course, I knew what it was. A rare cabochon emerald, fully six inches long and almost half as wide, it was carved into a likeness of the goddess Kali. She was delicately mounted in an ivory frame. The play of light through the jewel made it seem alive. Uncle Coe didn't answer when Grandfather asked where it came from, and I never heard him ask again.

Uncle Coe wasn't a real uncle. He'd been a close friend of my parents and after their deaths had always helped Grandfather look after me. He'd been pleased with my interest in India. He was proud when I was made curator of the University Museum and that I'd managed it successfully along with my other work.

I had just finished cataloging his collection and the Sheridan and university lawyers were drawing up the papers to make it legal. Now I wouldn't be here for the festivities. I knew that Uncle Coe was as disappointed as I was. Bill Holmes would have to take charge of it himself.

Bill was Uncle Coe's secretary and assistant who had been with him many years. He was making his own plans to return to India after the ceremony for some new and special acquisition of Uncle Coe's. I didn't know what, and they were unduly secretive about it. Uncle Coe had said only, "You'll never believe it until you see it, Bevan. The most exquisite thing ever to come out of India— Nepal—" he changed quickly.

I looked at them curiously. "Which do you mean— India or Nepal?"

Uncle Coe shrugged and Bill changed the subject, saying with no great enthusiasm, "I'll meet you in Kataipur sometime around Diwali." I wondered why he couldn't carry the message to Elizabeth, then remembered that there was no love lost between Miss Edith Dameron and Uncle Coe. And for some reason Miss Dameron was in a big hurry to get me to India.

Bill Holmes was the last person with whom I wanted to celebrate the Festival of Lights in Kataipur or anywhere else. He was gross—not fat but soft. He had a round, seamless face with wide china-blue eyes and a rubbery mouth with thick lips. His hands were square and thick, and the big ruby on his left hand looked almost obscene. A natty dresser, he leaned toward flashy jackets and silk shirts with ascots or turtleneck sweaters. He usually had a gold chain with a Greek or Egyptian amulet around his neck.

But there was one thing about Bill Holmes: he knew his business. In anything concerning antiquities, especially the Far East and India, he was a recognized authority.

Although, truth to tell, I had disagreed with him a number of times, I never proved him wrong. We were incompatible in a mild sort of way, but never let our differences show around Uncle Coe. In all fairness I think Bill was completely loyal to him.

I turned down the dark street that led past the Sheridan mansion and parked in front of the huge iron gates. Shuffling through leaves that should have been raked and hadn't, I walked up the steps to the high galleried porch with its spindled balustrade and faintly glowing fanlight. I reached to ring the bell, then decided to go in. He would probably be having dinner and there was no need to disturb Bertha. The door was unlocked. The hall was dimly lighted and through the double opening into the library I could see Uncle Coe. His elbow rested on the mantel and he was talking to someone out of my sight. His voice rose and his face looked flushed in the firelight. Then I recognized the crisp accent of the Hindu, Pita-Singh, as he interrupted.

"I'm sorry you see fit to ignore the seriousness of these charges. But make no mistake, Mr. Sheridan—if I'm forced to get a court order to prevent the transfer of your collection to the university, I shall. As for Mr. Holmes, keep him out of India." He moved into the doorway where I saw him, a tall silhouette, one hand in his pocket. I could hear the nervous jingle of coins as he bowed slightly. "Good evening, Mr. Sheridan."

Uncle Coe faced him slowly and deliberately. His hands were clenched, his feet defiantly apart, and his eyebrows fairly quivered with fury as he answered in a glacial tone, "Your court order be damned, sir!"

I slipped out of sight behind a multiheaded bronze Vishnu as Pita-Singh stepped into the hall. When I heard the front door close, I walked into the library. Uncle Coe had turned back to face the fire, his hands clasped behind him, his head bowed.

"What was that all about?" I asked.

He swung around quickly, his face lighted up. But anger was deeply imprinted on it. "Bevan, I'm damn glad to see you. I was afraid you'd leave without saying goodbye."

"You know better than that." I reached up on tiptoe to kiss his cheek. "Your friend who just left is the same one who covets my Deccan *Katar*—"

"No friend of mine, by God! He covets every damn thing I've got. And the SOB had the gall to threaten Bill if he goes to India."

"Bill?" I repeated. Harmless Bill Holmes would be the last person I'd expect to be threatened by anyone.

"He said he wouldn't guarantee Bill's safety if he returned to India. And I said the hell with that—I wasn't asking for any guarantee from him or anyone else."

"Well, good for you."

"Son of a bitch," he muttered, "son of a bitchen-wog —the British were the only people who knew how to handle them. . . ." He kept talking to himself under his breath while he filled his pipe and then motioned me to sit across from him. He sat down in the old wing chair.

"Are you going to tell Bill?" I asked.

He snorted. "It's not that important. Anyway, Bill's already gone." Then seeing my surprise he added, "It's that thing, an old temple sculpture—priceless. We've run into complications."

"But the showing—"

"It's more important to get this out—it's not as easy as it used to be. Bill knows you'll be in Kataipur and will look you up. He might even help you find something for the university. I hear the old lady is being pretty liberal with her money on this trip. . . ." There was a sound of irony, but when I looked up he winked. "Now buzz Bertha. You'll join me for dinner. Right now, though, you can mix us both a Scotch and soda."

I mixed the drinks, smiled when Bertha entered, and asked her if I might stay for dinner.

"Well, you just better. Your last night here—"

We were rather silent during the meal. Uncle Coe, I'm sure, was thinking about the brash Hindu, and I about this journey for which I had no enthusiasm. "You know," I said, reaching for another roll, "I've never heard you mention Kataipur, yet so many of your finest things came from there. What's it like?"

"Those 'things,' Bevan, were purchased through an agent. I was only there one time, and that was many years ago. So I really can't tell you what it's like. Far off the tourist track—a valley in the Himalayan foothills."

"Well, I'll find out soon enough and I'll let you know."

"Do that," he answered, and our dinner table conversation petered out.

Afterward we sat by the dying fire, Uncle Coe and I, nursing brandies, not talking. Then suddenly he said, "Bevan, it's time you got married!"

"Well, look who's talking!" I threw a small log on the fire and watched the sparks explode and eddy behind the screen until the flame, with its hydra-headed snakes' tongues, pushed them up the chimney.

"It's 'who's talking' that you should listen to." He dug his pipe into the humidor, tamped it firmly, and lighted it with intense concentration. He puffed a time or two until it was drawing properly, then leaned back in his chair and looked at me from under his bushy brows.

"Being in love was the main thing in my life when I was young. But the loves came too easily and died as quickly. Then the real thing came along and I almost didn't recognize it." He looked toward the fire and for a second or two he seemed a thousand miles away. If I hadn't known him so well I'd have said there was a mistiness in his eyes. "I couldn't—I didn't fight hard enough for her—and I guess I didn't deserve her. Bevan, you haven't fallen in love yet—but I want you to. And when it comes, don't let it slip through your fingers because you're more interested in a career of Indian antiquities!"

I laughed and placed my brandy glass on the coffee table. "Well, who would ever have thought you were an old softy under all that crust!"

He didn't smile. Regarding me seriously, he said, "Bevan, you worry me. You haven't a sentimental streak anywhere in your makeup. You're just all professor . . . do you suppose you are frigid?"

I flared then. "That's none of your goddamn business."

"Okay, okay, you're right. It's none of my damn business, but I've known you for a hell of a long time, and you should have been in love a dozen times or more. In school you were too interested in books. Now you're an authority on Indian art, you've a doctorate, a published textbook, and by God, what really do you have?"

I stood up and looked down at him coldly. "I'll tell you what I've got—a nice apartment where I can come and go as I please. I've a priceless Deccan dagger. I've worlds of friends and this is one goddamn conversation. I'm going home. Good night!"

His brows bristled as he stood up, but didn't hide the glitter in his eyes. "One of these days you'll be stunned by a bolt of lightning and a thunderclap, then go hog-wild over some guy who can tie you in knots and make you like it."

I stood at the door glaring at him. "Do you want to bet on it?"

"Damn right." His lids half hid his eyes. "The Emerald Kali."

"The Emerald Kali!" I took a quick breath. "The thought of having that—"

"If you're going to live alone all your life you'll need it." Then an odd grin creased his face. "The Emerald Kali against your Deccan *Katar.*"

I released my breath in a drawn-out whistle, then crossed back to where he stood and held out my hand. "It's a bet. You can kiss your Kali good-bye."

"What about the time limit?" he asked.

"A year," I said brightly.

"Hell, no!" he replied. "If you're so sexless that you can go for almost thirty years without bending, you'd go another year just for the Kali. Five years. But you have to be honest with me, girl. Even if it doesn't work out and you're run through a wringer, come tell me—hear?"

I laughed and kissed him on the cheek. "You're hedging your bet already. But I hear."

"And," he continued, "if I'm not around then, and God knows there's a chance—I'm hanging on Satan's limb and he has a sharp saw—you're still to be honest with me."

"It's not Satan's limb you're on, it's the good Lord's own, and you'll be around to personally hand me the Kali —may I see it again?"

He left the library and returned in a few minutes with the emerald goddess.

Carved from one incredible cabochon emerald, framed in ivory that had been incised with gold tendrils and tiny inlaid gem flowers, she was unbelievably exquisite and at the same time frightening. One didn't look at the Kali and smile. Her tongue stuck out; in one of her four hands she held a severed head by the scalp lock and in the opposite a scimitar; the others were raised in a blessing. A necklace of skulls swung around her neck to the hem of her skirt, and symbolic Man, entwined with a sacred Naga—a cobra—was supine beneath her foot. It was easy to understand why she was the symbol of life and death in one spirit goddess. There was no way one could look at her and not be moved.

The clear green stone was faintly traced with delicate flaws that threaded the gem like living arteries and gave it a feeling of life and movement as the firelight danced through it. I thought again, as I always did when I saw the Kali, of the truths, the half-truths, the myths of the emerald. I understood why it had rivaled the diamond in beauty and value through the ages. This was a living thing, a goddess emanating life, pulsing in my hands. I remembered that ancient pharmacists had used the gem to cure diseased parts of the body; that it was a charm against snakes; that it stimulated all appetites. I knew it was believed by the ancients that an emerald on the finger would burn when poison was near; that it calmed storms at sea, foreshadowed future events, revealed truths, conferred riches, joy, strength, virility, health. Certainly it had been important in all religions. It was one of the foundation stones of the New Jerusalem; the first Mohammedan heaven was an emerald, and in India it assured knowledge of the soul, the value of human existence —karma. Undoubtedly the ancient sculptor who carved this gemstone had understood all of these things, and he gave these lasting truths life in this green goddess of destruction.

I cradled her in both hands, staring at the magic of

her winking, evil body. "She is worth a lifetime of celibacy," I whispered.

"We'll find out," the old man answered.

I placed her on the coffee table in front of the fireplace where she caught the flickering glow and returned flame for flame. And without taking my eyes from her, I reached into my bag for the Deccan *Katar*. I handed it to Uncle Coe. "There's really no comparison. This is probably worth fifty or a hundred thousand against a couple of million." I reached for the Kali again.

He smiled at me saying, "Well, together they make a king's ransom. Or should we say a maharaja's?"

I nodded. There was no doubt in my mind that here were two of the most beautiful works of art in the world. "Worth—well, worth five years' waiting," I added.

"You and your grandfather are the only persons who have seen her since—since she was given to me."

"How long ago was that?"

He looked into the fire and then at me. His smile was a faraway one. "So long ago, Bevan—"

"And the person who gave her to you," I persisted. "A woman?"

His face relaxed and his eyes softened. "Yes," he answered, speaking so low that I moved closer to hear him. "Yes, a woman—a very special woman." He paused a long time before he added, "When love is real, the memory is long—so now we'll speak no more of it." He touched the curve of the ivory frame and, changing the subject, said, "Wouldn't Bill go crazy over her?"

"You mean Bill's never seen her?" I was naturally surprised.

"No, nor anyone else. The Kali is not something to be placed on exhibition."

He was right. The Kali was not an idle gem to be

devoured by curious eyes. Somehow I was glad that Bill didn't know about her. I ran my hands over the stone, then took the soft cloth she had been wrapped in and wiped away my fingerprints. I returned her to Uncle Coe. "Had you realized that Dussehra—the festival of Kali— is just over?"

He nodded. "Yes. It varies—it's always set by the astrologers. Sometimes they have a hard time agreeing." He tapped his pipe against his hand, emptying it into the fireplace, then replaced it in a rack with half a dozen others, at the same time saying, "I'd like to see the celebrations again, the performance of the Ram-Lila, always in an open-air theater, and afterward the fireworks—and on the tenth day the burning of the demon kings and Rama shooting a fire arrow into Ravana's effigy. The final triumph of good over evil."

"And if the Kali temples run with blood most of the time—think what Dussehra means, in sacrifices!" I was remembering the Kali temple in Calcutta.

"Yes, it's a sight to see. The kneeling women with a tilak of blood between their brows, the flowers at the feet of the goddess—"

"It's almost pagan," I said. "Still, it's spiritual too. I never did get used to the sight and smell of the blood. But it's like the Old Testament, with their ritual sacrifices. . . ." Then I added, "Thank goodness it's only sheep and goats and chickens."

He looked at me with an odd expression in his eyes. "Bevan, do you really think the day of human sacrifice is over?"

"Of course," I answered, wondering if he was making a joke. But he wasn't.

"Then you don't know your India as well as you think."

I wanted to laugh at his seriousness. Instead I smiled and shook my head. "That's where you're wrong, Uncle Coe. I know my India and yours and Indira Gandhi's better than you do. Modern India is as far removed from the India you knew as medieval times from today."

"That's not a very apt analogy." He motioned with the Kali. "I think you'll be surprised at the power embodied in this goddess."

I grinned and threw my coat over my shoulders. "You lived in India too long."

"What you're really thinking is that I'm getting senile."

"God forbid! You'll never be senile—but superstitious, yes. You've brought superstitions back with you, and like shades of the dead you can't—or you don't want to—be rid of them."

He shrugged. "Perhaps you're right. Well, the Kali goes in the lockbox tomorrow and the *Katar* will keep her company. Good-bye, Bevan, have a good trip and don't let Bill bug you!"

I laughed. "He'd bug a saint. But I'll try to endure him, and perhaps he'll give me a few leads on some goodies for the museum."

"If anyone can, it's Bill." He kissed me on the cheek and saw me to the door. "Remember our pact with the Kali."

"Do you think I could ever forget!" He closed the door softly behind me and I left the old Sheridan mansion with a warm feeling. How dear of Uncle Coe. My throat tightened at the thought of owning the Kali.

Quite a group was gathered at the airport to see me off the next morning. There was Lane Thomas, but we hardly spoke. Bertha was there and several of my students who figured this would surely be an excused cut. Miss Edith Dameron was there full of last-minute advice. "Call me as soon as you see Elizabeth!" "I will, Miss Edith, I will." "No, tell her to call me!" "I will, Miss Edith!" Then she kissed me, and Lane kissed me, and Bertha kissed me. I drew the line with the students, but I don't think that was in their plans anyway.

Just before the plane was announced, Uncle Coe came up. Before he spoke to me he took Miss Edith's hand and smiled at her. "It's been a long time, Edith."

"Hello, Corraway," she replied vaguely, turning back to me. "Don't forget, Bevan."

"No, Miss Edith. That's why I'm going, remember?" My question was facetious and I was ashamed as soon as I said it. They called the flight. I kissed Uncle Coe quickly, blew a kiss over my shoulder, and escaped as quickly as I could into the plane.

Settling myself into a window seat, I leaned back, glad that I couldn't see any of them. Good-byes were boring. Certainly there's nothing worse than standing around waiting for the departure of a plane, a train, or a carload of guests. I was glad that Uncle Coe came. It was the first time I'd ever seen him and Miss Edith together. I figured they were about the same age. Her voice changed when he spoke to her. It was high and cold, like the nervous chirp of a sparrow. I touched my tongue to the corner of my mouth. It felt dry. All that kissing. I pulled my compact from my purse and ran a bit of color over my lips, then took a second look at my reflection.

My hair waved loose in a shoulder bob; it was a rather ordinary shade of brown. My eyes were that sort of hazel that comes from a blue-eyed father and a brown-eyed mother, and goes naturally with an olive skin. My chin was too pointed and my eyebrows didn't match. I squinted and looked at the image that stared back at me with a critical eye. All in all I wasn't bad looking. And for almost thirty —how did they say?—damn well preserved! There was a no-nonsense set to my mouth, but four years of outwitting college students could account for that. I smiled at the mirror—just to see what I looked like smiling—and somehow the transformation intrigued me. When ever had I smiled before, for no reason at all? My face softened and I looked rather pretty. Then like a smash of thunder on a clear day I heard, "As the poet said, 'Vanity, vanity, thy name is woman—' "

I snapped the compact shut and felt my face flame. The hardest thing I ever did was to turn and look up at the tall Hindu. His face was camouflaged by dark sunglasses. He stood in the aisle folding his trench coat into the overhead rack. Then he looked down at me with a lopsided grin that was completely unnatural on his face, and jackknifed his long legs into the aisle seat. I dropped the compact into my purse and said ineptly, "Oh, hello. It's Mr. Pita-Singh, isn't it?"

"I think, Dr. Blakley, you know well enough it's Mr. Pita-Singh," he answered, fastening his seat belt. "Why did you take the *Katar* out of the museum?" The plane began to move away from the terminal.

"What makes you think I took it?" I asked innocently.

"No one else would. Besides, you left a small clue. A note with your initials. Which part do you plan to repair?"

"Well, it's none of your concern, Mr. Pita-Singh." I shrugged, withdrawing into my corner, and opened a magazine. "If you'll excuse me now," I said without looking at him, "I've an article here. . . ."

He didn't answer, but took a magazine himself. However, as soon as we were airborne he tipped back his seat, let the magazine drop to the floor, and fell asleep.

After several minutes my curiosity was more than I could manage, so I closed the magazine and twisted in my seat so I could look at him—discreetly. There was a stubborn look about his chin, a firmness that showed even in the strength of his neck. He looked like a man who would make no idle threats. I wondered how old he was. Probably thirty-two or -three, perhaps even older. At any rate he carried an air of authority.

If he could stand up to Uncle Coe, who was no mild antagonist himself, he would certainly go to any length to secure the Deccan *Katar*. He had an unusual name, Pita-Singh. The literal translation was "Father of a Lion." It would be interesting to know how that came about. It's only recently that Indians have used family names—and that is usually for reasons of caste. Singh, I knew, was probably the most common name in India. All Sikhs carry it, but this man wasn't a Sikh. That sect never cut their hair, twisting it and their beard under a turban. They carried a dagger, wore a steel bracelet and special undershorts which, I smiled to myself, I'd never had occasion to see. Certainly this man was no Sikh.

He was clean-shaven, his lips thin, his cheekbones high. His complexion was a rich tan that showed hours in the sun. Thick eyebrows arched partially above sunglasses and his hair fell across his forehead in a careless sort of way. Even asleep, there was nothing about him that looked friendly or relaxed. Then I wondered perversely if the grim line that seamed his left cheek hadn't been a dimple when he was a child. Certainly he was handsome in a "life is serious, life is earnest" way. Suddenly he reached up, took off his glasses, and stared at me. I felt a slow flush roll across my face, but I was unable to take my eyes away from his. They never seemed to be the same shade—now they were a sort of topaz. He had a natural squint with crosshatch wrinkles that belong to men who are much in the sunlight: sailors and hunters and ranchers. His face was hawklike, lean and hungry looking, and I broke away from his gaze with an almost visible effort, to pick up my magazine.

"Why did you hide behind the Vishnu last night?" he asked abruptly.

"Hide behind the Vishnu?" I repeated stupidly.

"At Mr. Sheridan's." He shifted in his chair so that he was looking directly at me with his strange-colored eyes. "Dr. Blakley, why are you afraid of me?"

I sat up straight at that and replied in a voice chilly with dignity, "Afraid! You're rather ridiculous, Mr.—Mr.—"

"Pita-Singh. You were eavesdropping."

"I was not!"

"I hope you heard enough that you will convince Sheridan he should return his collection to the Indian government. He's heading for trouble."

"Are you threatening Mr. Sheridan?"

"Dr. Blakley, I'm concerned with getting property back that belongs to India. Artifacts that were stolen from my country—"

"That is a threat!"

"It depends on how you take it. I'm afraid Mr. Sheridan didn't consider it one."

"And you threatened Bill. I heard you!"

"If you took it as a threat, perhaps he will also, and stay away from India. We are bloody well tired of having state treasures taken out of the country. I'm going to stop it."

"Legally or illegally—it makes no difference?"

"It depends on one's point of view, Dr. Blakley."

The announcement to straighten our seats and fasten our belts came over the speaker. We were making our descent into Washington. "You're going on to New York?" he asked.

I nodded. If he didn't know I was going to India, there was no point in telling him. He gathered up his briefcase and his coat. As he moved down the aisle he turned and glanced back briefly. "I'd watch that Narcissus syndrome. It can be a deadly affliction."

"You should know better than anyone," I answered. No question about it. He was a hell of a disagreeable man.

chapter III

As the big plane swung into its landing pattern at the Palam airport, I had my nose glued to the window. It was just as it had been before, the flight from Rome across the Mediterranean, at such an altitude that there was nothing except layered cumulus cotton fluff below. Once the clouds parted to reveal the Persian mountains, then closed like a theater curtain not to open again until the overture was played and Delhi in its vast red desert mounting broke into view. The runway rose rapidly to meet us and the plane rolled to a stop outside the terminal.

Heat hovered above the macadam apron in simmering waves thick with the smell of oil and asphalt. The glare bounced off the wing and seared my face as I stood in the doorway of the plane waiting to descend. Shielding my eyes, I looked over the passengers strung out from the plane to the building. Indian dress, Western clothes, African robes swirled together in a melange of colors. In the airport, slow-moving ceiling fans stirred thick humid air with a soft whirring sound. The bright wash of saris, the oiled slick black hair, tight half-blouses with quarter moons of perspiration stains circling underarms, dark slender men in wilted muslin shirts, dhotis, crumpled jodhpurs, turbans, and Nehru caps—a tide of leather-colored men and women enveloped me in a noisy human exuberance that I'd not felt before.

Ubiquitous sweepers moved crab-like on their haunches across the dusty floor, mechanically working their twig brooms with no degree of enthusiasm. Dressed in dirt-gray turbans and dhotis, they were the untouchables whom Gandhi called *Harijan*—God's people. But were they? Passengers circled them as carelessly as they would detour a bench or a post. The blank expressions on their faces showed a dogged determination to see this life out and the next lived in the mold for which it was created, without question or ambition. It was a face formed to its mask of patient endurance, speaking of an India that hadn't touched me before.

I passed through customs preoccupied with my thoughts. Six years ago I'd been met by a welcoming delegation from the university, hurried through a VIP customs and on to the hotel in a private car. I hadn't had time to see, or hear, or smell, or to feel the India that whirled about me now.

Gathering my luggage and waving away hordes of porters wanting to help, I found a bench and sat down. I had only an hour to catch the plane to Kataipur. Still I sat. I had planned to take the plane to Kataipur, say "Hello" and "Please write your auntie" to Elizabeth, then catch the first plane back to Delhi and the States. And if that was too soon to suit Lane Thomas, then he could take Miss Dameron's endowments and lump them! I made a damn poor cat's-paw.

But now, sitting in the terminal building, I was seeing an India that was strange to me—and I didn't understand. Had I forgotten so completely, or had I never known?

What had absorbed me in my two years, so that I'd skimmed over a very real part of India? Had I been so involved in the study of Sanskrit and Hindi that I had had no time to involve myself with the people? Had the study of Indian art, history, and philosophy meant only a superficial culture that I would transfer to other students as unaware as I? Had Elizabeth felt this? The other Sheridan scholars?

It took only minutes to cancel my flight to Kataipur. Elizabeth could wait. I would revisit old haunts, perhaps find someone I'd known. I needed to put myself at ease in what should have been comfortable surroundings but somehow weren't. I needed a different perspective, and I would take time to find it. Why did I have this strange feeling that I'd never been here before?

I made reservations at the Rayson Hotel for a deluxe room for a week. With Miss Edith Dameron footing my bill, I should enjoy this first part of my Indian vacation, even if the last part choked me.

The taxi ride to the hotel was just as I remembered, and the nearer to the city the faster became the left-handed traffic. I'd have to get used to that again. The parched red earth with spots of irrigated green, the riding academy where I'd spent Saturday afternoons, the oversize billboards advertising Indian movies, young trees with wire fences or oil drums to protect them from roaming cattle, the traffic circle, past Embassy Road, the Maidan, then the circled drive into the hotel. I'd stayed there before when I began my studies, and no part of it had changed. That was reassuring. There was a different clerk behind the desk, but he welcomed me with a warm smile. Suddenly I had an easy feeling of stepping back in time—into a familiar niche. The strangeness left and I felt at home.

I followed the porter to my room. He settled my luggage and pulled up the blinds. After I tipped him and closed the door behind him, I stretched the weariness out of my muscles and leaned over the window ledge. A garden was below, lovely with paths, clipped lawns, and lush flowers. Black-leafed mango trees and lazy acacias drooping in the afternoon heat accented the garden with purple shadows and made it appear cooler than it was.

As quickly as that I began to find myself. India was here, all about me. In the garden and its flowers, in the deep shade, in the smiling hospitality of the clerk and the bearer. Not the India I'd felt at the airport, but the one I had known. It was here and I'd have no trouble finding it again. I felt a certain exhilaration. And if I felt a tinge of conscience about Elizabeth, I buried it quickly enough. I bathed and dressed and went to the bar.

I picked up an English language newspaper from the desk clerk, then found the bar hidden in a dark corner of the lobby. Pale little lamps with parchment shades cast an orange circle in the center of each table and gave barely enough light to read. I had the bar entirely to myself. I ordered a whiskey and soda, then settled down to see what there'd be to do that evening. I passed over the front page and folded the paper to the entertainment section, spreading it flat on the table under the circle of light. The lead story had a picture of the star and an explanation of why the Ram-Lila—that favorite of all Indian folk-religious legends which I knew well—would be repeated so soon after Dussehra. Some visiting dignitaries from Russia had expressed a desire to see the famous production and there would be a special performance at an outdoor theater. That was pure luck and certainly not to be missed.

Pleased that my plans for the evening had jelled so quickly, I made a mental note to check out the museum and the university the next morning for old acquaintances. I glanced rapidly through the rest of the paper. My drink came as I reached the front page. The headlines were bleak. Cyclone havoc in Orissa; whole villages swept away; Paradip port put out of commission. There was the crisis along the border; Pak guns in Sylhit hammered Tripura border towns; Indira Gandhi in Europe explaining India's position on Bangladesh; plague in Tamil Nadu. Much news and all of it bad. No different, I thought, from the States. Just a different kind of bad news.

Then my eye was drawn to a small boxed item in the center of the page, cut in two by the perimeter of light. I read it through slowly, unbelieving, then refolded the paper so I could see it better, pushed it farther under the light and read again—shocked, still unbelieving.

It was a six-inch column with an insignificant small-cap head that read: CHILD SACRIFICE CASE and under that in blacker type *Father and Son Remanded.* But it was the article that captured my full attention. Beside the indented dateline the story began. In the ambiguous journalistic prose common in English-language Indian papers I read: *Saran Pathak, a DTU conductor, who had been arrested here yesterday along with his father on the charge of sacrificing his four-year-old son at the altar of Goddess Kali during the recent Dussehra festival, was produced before the additional district magistrate (North). They were remanded to the custody of the police for a week. Later both of them will be taken to Kataipur where they will be tried on charges of murder, criminal intimidation and concealment of crime.*

I swallowed hard, took a quick breath and continued reading: *Witnesses said that Pathak performed the ritual murder because he had been instructed in a dream by the*

Goddess Kali that by such sacrifice the Emerald Goddess would be restored to the Kali Temple at Kataipur. Pathak father and son were born in Kataipur province but have lived in Delhi for several years. Pathak senior was a priest at the Kali Temple at one time.

It wasn't until I pushed the paper back and sank against my chair that I realized I was holding my breath. The *Emerald Kali!* There couldn't be two of them. I remembered holding the jewel Kali and thinking of her as though she was alive. And—was it only last night, the night before?—half a world away, Uncle Coe had asked me if I thought that only animals were used in ritual sacrifices. I wondered if I'd laughed.

No, I hadn't laughed—nothing that has to do with the Goddess Kali is a laughing matter—but I'd said he was wrong. That he didn't understand the New India. The advanced thinking. The cultural achievements. My God! How wrong could I be? Here on the front page of a Delhi paper in this splendid year of our Lord . . . Goose bumps rode my shoulders. Of course the man was mad. But there it was in a little boy's blood—the dark side of the coin. And when I was here before I'd never even felt it.

I pushed the drink aside; it tasted bitter. I signed the check, rolled up the paper and stuck it under my arm, and went back to my room. I was glad when evening came and I could go to the Ram-Lila.

It was just as well that I knew the story by heart, because I couldn't keep my mind on it. Every Hindu child is raised on the story of Lord Rama from the epic *Ramayana*. It's the national bedtime story, the inspiration for the finest Indian sculpture and painting, and it was written between 500 and 100 B.C. In this perfect love story, Rama is cast as the ideal son, brother, husband, and although he distrusts Sita, his wife, for a while, it all ends happily enough. His name is uttered twice in the greeting *Ram Ram,* and in times of great stress. *"Eh, Ram!"* were the last words spoken by Mahatma Gandhi at the moment of his assassination. With one part of my mind I thought of the frightened, bewildered little boy whose blood was to appease the goddess of destruction, and with the other I felt the rhythm of the chants, watched the dramatic dancing, listened to the story as it was sung by the musicians who squatted almost unseen in the shadows.

And still I remembered the Emerald Kali. Above the rhythm of the chanting and the music it passed through my mind that I'd give anything to return the Kali to the temple where it belonged. Suddenly my throat was dry and I felt a sickening wave of nausea. All the lights on the stage fused together with the brilliant costumes in a psychedelic haze, and I put my hand to my head and closed my eyes until the dizziness passed. After a few minutes I was all right. No—not all right.

I was rocked on my own foundation at such a thought. Had the ritual sacrifice of the little boy been successful? If I . . . if I planned to return the Emerald Kali to the Kataipur temple, did that mean a fulfillment of the sacrifice? I felt the sweat, cold and wet, on the nape of my neck.

That night I slept restlessly. Skimming along the edge of my consciousness was the nightmare of the child. I was glad when morning came.

None of my old acquaintances were in Delhi. They were scattered all over the East. The museum director was out of town for two weeks. So sorry. Perhaps on your next visit. . . .

I wished that the Sheridan Fellowship Scholar had chosen Delhi instead of Madras for his final year of study. I needed someone—anyone I could talk to. I shrugged off my growing despondency and rented a car. Perhaps revisiting those places I'd known so well could take some of the stickiness away from the newspaper item, since it is the nature of us all to forget the unpleasant. At any rate I pushed it back in my mind, hoping it would stay buried beneath all the sightseeing I intended to pile on top of it.

I went first to the well-remembered tomb of Humayun with its moorish arches, its charming three-layered-cake look. I wandered around the Jantar Mantar, that astronomical jigsaw puzzle designed with such skill that today, two hundred and fifty years later, it tells the exact hour on its great stone clock face and all the movements of the stars. I spent hours at the Red Fort, enjoying as I always had the fragile beauty of its marble fretwork and decorative inlay in the walls and ceilings. I revisited the Birla Temple where Gandhi was shot and his monument that marks the place of his cremation where the words *"Eh, Ram!"* are carved at one end of the stone slab. Gandhi, whose memory will never die, whose dreams for a better life for the untouchables were made into law—but can any legal order change the prejudices of centuries?

I wandered around the circular Parliament House, had a drink at the Ashoka Hotel Bar. I knew my way around the Connaught Circus and found it hadn't changed as much as I'd expected. The road was still filled with taxis, horse carts, gharries, bicycle tongas, fancifully decorated trucks, children, men, women, workmen carrying goatskins filled with water sprinkling down the dust, and everywhere cattle wandering at will. Delhi had something of a village atmosphere, and its charm enfolded me as it had done before.

I bought crewel and brocades and silk saris and had them mailed home. I searched for antiques—but there were none of museum value. Not even behind the counters of export shops or under the tables of the temples where I knew there had been surreptitious dealings in the past.

There was simply no link now to a Brahman priest who would be willing to part with ancient sculptures or ritual bells. Traffic in Indian antiquities was drying up and I asked why. "Ah, Madame, it is the government. They are very strict now about exporting anything—even duplications, even new copies."

Well, if I couldn't find anything here there would be Kataipur, and Bill, of course. Then I remembered the Hindu, Pita-Singh, whose mission in life was to save Indian antiquities. Very noble of him. But he should know that they have better care in Britain and the States. Not only that, I would give him fair warning, if he were here, that I'd bring back to Midwestern University Museum anything of value I could find. And when the newspaper clipping and the memory of the sweepers crossed my mind, I pigeonholed them neatly in a far corner of my brain. The little boy and his foolish father were imprinted on another leaf in a manuscript too thick, too deep, too intricate to involve me. God knows every country has a dark side where rough edges unravel themselves at times. Why should I let it disturb me? I wouldn't be here that long. I'd go see Elizabeth, deliver my message, and catch the next flight back to New York. I would return to teaching oriental art, making restorations and appraisals of collections and I'd never—*I'd never return to India.*

Suddenly I had a frantic desire to leave Delhi and be done with my commission. Back at the hotel I found that the plane to Kataipur flew only once a week—that was yesterday, the flight I'd cancelled. But there was a train leaving at six the following morning which would put me in Darampur. From there I could make connections to Kataipur. Even though it would be an all-day trip, that would be better than waiting almost a week for another plane.

Delhi Junction, at six in the morning, had all the

wild color and sound of a movie set. I found my compartment, letting a porter from the hotel who had gotten my ticket for me run interference, and settled down into the old-fashioned plush seat that scratched through my shirt. Even at that hour the atmosphere was stifling and pressed close around me, disturbed only a fraction by a slow-moving overhead fan. I opened the window, but it was no better. The air was thick and stagnant around the train, bruised by the heavy odor of axle grease and steam and creosoted ties, stirred a little perhaps by the crush of people shouting and pushing and elbowing their way up and down the platform, around inert bundles of white-swathed bodies asleep wherever the mood struck them to lie down.

I had the compartment to myself and for that I was grateful. But it seemed all the people weren't going my direction. Other trains on other tracks were literally inhaling the crowd in fast-moving streams. I heard the whistle and felt the quick jerk and the oiled smoothness of the wheels. The train moved away from the station slowly at first, then faster, the wheels clicking an increasing cadence. I watched sari-clad women fuse together in a rainbow blur of waving hands shouting farewells and wondered that they could be so enthusiastic at such an early hour. Grimy buildings slipped by quickly, and busy intersections where wooden rails bunched tongas and bullock carts and brown-skinned people in spotless white behind them—all the frantic early-morning traffic.

I melted into a corner of the compartment, stretched my feet on the opposite seat, and let my body roll with the motion of the train. I felt an undisguised relief at leaving Delhi. Then I was surprised to realize that I was looking forward to seeing Elizabeth.

The sun came up out of the eastern sky in a quick

blinding burst that turned long parallels of track into streaks of fire and reflected our passing in the gold-flecked windows of empty cars along the sidings. A fast-moving shadow appeared alongside, undulating with the terrain, now long and exaggerated, bumping over ties, now short and disappearing beneath a cinder embankment, moving with a rhythm of its own seemingly independent of the train.

Then we were away from Delhi on the vast red desert plain that surrounds it. I dozed off and woke up as we were pulling into Panjadu, the only stop between Delhi and Darampur. The train slowed, came to a lurching, squeaking halt, and immediately floods of passengers fell off to surround a tea vendor. He had a wooden tray filled with earthenware cups balanced precariously on his head. I watched as he wiped out cups with a grubby cloth, then filled them from an oversized metal teapot. Other vendors were shouting *"Narangi, narangi, acche acche narangi!"*— oranges, oranges, good, good oranges. I followed the passengers out and bought three of them and a bottle of water, then climbed back into my compartment.

I was peeling an orange when suddenly through my open window I heard, above the hubbub of shouting passengers and crying vendors, a voice—a woman's voice—say in Hindi: "Is the American princess the one?" And another woman answered her. "No one really knows. No more, of course, than one knows about the prince."

I sat up straight, straining my ears to hear. The first woman then said, "She can take comfort in the words of Krishna to Arjuna—*Who thinks that he has slain, Cannot then understand, He slays not—nor is slain—*" And the other voice broke in quickly, "It is written truly and well said: *What is can never disappear. . . .*"

The words made no sense, yet I held them in my mind

while I opened the door and stepped onto the platform searching for the speakers. It was filled with both men and women crisscrossing in every direction. It could have been any of the sari-clad women with the bright tilak between their brows, but although I looked and listened, I heard neither voice again. When the conductor blew his whistle I re-entered the compartment.

What had the women been talking about? The American princess would have to be Elizabeth. And I knew they were quoting the *Bhagavad-Gita* and its not-so-subtle theme of reincarnation. Who had died that now he lived again?

The train started; the station platform was almost deserted except for mail carts and the inevitable residue of relatives waving good-bye. I finished peeling the orange mechanically, then forgot to eat it. I sat there mile after mile trying to find an answer to the puzzle.

I knew as surely as if she had been called by name that the women were referring to Elizabeth Dameron—and I knew with a tightening in my heart that she was in some dreadful trouble.

Three hours later I climbed off what seemed to be a deserted train onto a deserted platform at Darampur. The lonely station was miles from the city, but I shouldn't have too long to wait. I found a bench, dug into my tote and pulled out the last of the oranges I'd bought in Panjadu. I'd just finished it when a ramshackle taxi careened into sight. The turbaned chauffeur braked it to a skidding, quivering halt near the station platform. He had an impressive beard and a steel bracelet dangling below the sleeve of his coat as he gestured from the window. I knew he was a Sikh, and that his name would be Singh. "I'll take you to Darampur—it's only fifteen minutes, Memsahib."

I shook my head. "No thank you. I'm taking the train to Kataipur this afternoon. I'll wait here."

"Kataipur!" he answered, clearly astonished that anyone would be going there. "Oh, but Memsahib, it's a long time—the train is hours late today. I will show you Darampur, then you can take the mail bus and get there much faster." He climbed out of the taxi and shoved my bag onto the front seat. I climbed in back; it was easier than arguing, and the sooner I got to Kataipur the better.

It was noon—and I was hungry. "Rather than a tour of your city," I said, "I'll settle for a good lunch.—"

"Right," he answered. "You will have a satisfactory luncheon at the Mount View Hotel, then I give you deluxe tour of Darampur." He turned, all business, and produced a card which read, *K. R. Singh, Guide, Interpreter, Business Consultant. Rates Hourly.* We settled on a satisfactory hourly rate until the estimated time of departure of the mail bus and then set out for the Mount View Hotel. I sank comfortably into a deep hollow in the back seat where countless posteriors before mine had broken down the springs.

It was cool, even at midday, and the faint feel of autumn in the Himalayan foothills was in the air.

We drove the fifteen miles into Darampur with my driver talking unceasingly. He covered the weather, the political situation, Indira Gandhi, and I sat back letting the sound of his voice roll about me.

It took longer to order and eat my lunch than it did to see all that I wanted to see of Darampur.

An hour later I suggested we find a protected corner of the bazaar, have a cup of hot tea, and wait for the mail car. I was tired of his running commentary on the bleak little city.

We had barely seated ourselves at a small table beneath a neem tree and ordered tea when he turned his one-sided conversation to Kataipur. "Few people go to Kataipur without reason," he began. "I think the Memsahib is going to see the American."

It was a flat unequivocal statement and I looked at him surprised. "Why—why should you think that?"

He shrugged. "Kataipur is not a tourist city—there is nothing there. So you must be going to see the American princess."

I hedged with a question. "Kataipur is near the mountains—why wouldn't it be a tourist city?"

The tea came in a heavy brass pot, and I poured. The Sikh thought for a minute and then said, "It has not caught up with the New India yet. It was one of the most isolated of the princely states, and the Maharaja is a very stubborn man. The law says his power is gone. Madame Prime Minister just last month changed all the princes to common men and took away their privy purses—just *Shri* now, not *Your Highness*—but the old Raja hasn't heard."

"I should think he'd hear when she cut off his privy purse."

"To a man like the Maharaja it means nothing. He has more investments abroad than he could count in lakhs. When he received the letter from the government stripping him of his title and purse he published a statement saying: '*My* relationship with *my* people is based on *my* family's ancient obligation to the state and to *my* people, and no amount of government action can ever change that.' You can be quite sure he will be called Highness until he dies." Then he spat. " '*My* people.' Like chattels, he speaks of us. . . ."

I wondered about his excellent English, at the same time wanting to switch the conversation around to Elizabeth without appearing curious.

I answered, "Surely the Maharaja would want to en-
courage tourists, especially since he's lost his privy purse.
It should bring some prosperity at least."

"No. Not at Kataipur. The Maharaja doesn't want
tourists."

I interrupted. "If that's so, then why would he turn
his Moti Palace into a hotel? That's where I'm staying."

"That wasn't his doing. The Moti Palace has tradi-
tionally belonged to the *Yuvraj*, the oldest son. Colonel
Durga only did what the Maharajas of Jaipur and Udaipur
and others have done, and found a source of income from
a hotel that used to be a palace. Americans, they say,
especially like that sort of thing. If we could get them
here. . . ."

"Who wouldn't," I countered, "like to live like a
maharaja for a few days?"

"Well, the Moti Palace in Kataipur isn't a Lake
Palace nor yet a Rambagh Palace, but it's still large enough
that it's never been filled to capacity. Kataipur is too far
out of the way and nothing has been done to attract tourists. The old Maharaja doesn't want them. He thinks
they'll spend too much money, tip too extravagantly, bring
dissension and make his—there's that possessive pronoun
again—people dissatisfied."

"Then it's strange he would send his sons to England
to be educated, feeling the way he does."

"Oh, the old Raja isn't stupid. He knows well enough
that to survive they had to cope with Europeans, Americans, and New India's politicians." He shrugged. "And
all for nothing—" Before I could ask him what he meant
he continued, "He knows that Kataipur will eventually be
opened up, but he'll delay it as long as possible. Right now
he's trying to prevent a travel writer from doing an article
about the beauties of undeveloped Kataipur." He stopped

and looked at me sideways. "I've been his guide. But the article will be published and then more travel writers will come and more articles will be written, and soon the Moti Palace Hotel will be booked for months ahead. The old Maharaja is fighting a losing battle. And certainly the dark times the astrologers predicted have come."

"Dark times?" I repeated.

"The accidents that have plagued the house. You don't know—about the sons? About the prince?"

Suddenly my throat felt dry. I shook my head. "What kind of accidents?"

"You haven't heard from the American princess? I thought that was why you were here."

"No," I answered, wishing he would get on with it. "What are you talking about?"

"Such tragedies. Colonel Durga, of course, was the heir. A colonel in the army. He was killed in a Pak border clash—"

"Would you call that an accident? I'd say rather it was an act of war. When did it happen?"

"A year ago when the young Rajasthan princess died."

I looked at him then—with interest. He caught my glance and nodded. "Yes, the one married to Prince Jai. Immediately afterwards he married the American . . . it was ill-advised."

"Why—ill-advised?"

"They married without consulting the court astrologers who know these things, who know when such events should take place."

"I don't believe in all that," I muttered.

He shrugged and emptied his cup and added abruptly, "The second son, Bhimi, was killed in a plane crash last summer, and the third son, Jai—"

"Yes—go on," I prompted when he hesitated, "what about Jai and Elizabeth?"

He fingered his bearded chin and looked at me. "That's why I thought you were here. You are a friend of the American?"

"Of course," I said impatiently.

"You don't know that he, her husband Jai, is dead by her hand?" His question was so soft, so unexaggerated, so understated that it took a full minute for his meaning to become clear. Even then I asked him again.

"What do you mean?"

"She killed him."

Just like that he said it. I knew he wasn't lying, that he believed what he was telling me. And I knew just as surely that he was mistaken. Suddenly the unclear reference to the *Bhagavad-Gita* became terribly explicit. I knew that the women, whoever they were, were just as mistaken as this man. I shook my head. "Oh, no. You're wrong. Elizabeth couldn't kill anyone—"

"But she did. The Maharaja's secretary came upon her afterwards while she still held the dagger."

I felt drained. I answered in a chalky voice, "That's not true. I know her."

He shrugged and stood up. "It's time to go. The mail bus will arrive soon." In almost an afterthought he asked, "Then you don't know about the young prince?"

I don't think I really heard his question. I stood up mechanically, my mind in a turmoil. He continued without waiting for my reply. "Prince Krishna was the only son of Colonel Durga; there are two sisters, I believe. After his father died Krishna was heir to the Ivory Throne —only ten years old. A month ago he died in the palace garden—it was a cobra."

--⟨ 47 ⟩--

I was as chilled as if I'd been wrapped in an arctic wind. "Oh, no—" I whispered.

"There are some superstitious people in Kataipur who even blame his death on the American."

I looked at him quickly. Suddenly everything settled into a new perspective. "That's ridiculous," I answered calmly enough.

"Of course it is," he replied. "But you must remember there are many people in India who still believe that disaster can come from a person simply because that person is a symbol of evil."

I looked him straight in the eyes and answered through clenched teeth. "Elizabeth could never be a symbol of evil. I know that she didn't kill her husband, no matter how many witnesses say she did!"

I had forgotten as quickly as that that I'd resented having to come to Kataipur. That I'd harbored a foolish animosity against her since I'd first seen her as a young college freshman. Now there was only a surging desire to help. "If what you say is true," I added, "the press would have headlined it around the world."

"You are right, Memsahib. That's why I was surprised when you said you were going to Kataipur. I thought the American princess had gotten word to you. It isn't generally known outside the palace."

I stopped him with an angry gesture and asked with low-voiced urgency, "Then why would you spread such stupid lies!"

"I swear by Guru Nanak's holy eyes what I say is truth, Memsahib. I come from Kataipur. My father, my grandfather, were in the service of the old Raja. My brother, Pandu, is chauffeur to His Highness. Is truth, Memsahib. But you will not repeat—I beg—you will not say you know K. R. Singh. I will go back some day. You understand?"

"Why did you tell me?"

"By my faith, Memsahib, I do not know. You must go now. Mail car is ready to leave."

Stunned, I opened my purse and paid him the rupees agreed. Then I followed him across the empty boulevard into a crush of people at the bus station. I shared the car with one other passenger, a white-bearded Sikh in an army uniform who climbed in after me. He smiled and said something in Punjabi, but I shook my head, as though I couldn't understand. I wanted no conversation. I'd had enough to ruin my trip to Kataipur and to make me wonder what I would face there.

K. R. Singh had told the truth as he understood it— at least as someone believed. If they thought Elizabeth had killed Jai, then where was she—in prison? Why were they being so secretive about it? Was justice, the old Maharaja's full-power, absolute-monarchy type of justice, going to be administered secretly?

The car creaked and chugged away from the Darampur station with a jolting, unwilling motor, and I wondered if we would ever get to Kataipur. A bleak countryside slipped past monotonously; the narrow road cut through a dusty country of red earth held together by scrubby bushes and scrawny trees and desert grass. There were occasional patches of green millet beside irrigation ditches where a yoked ox circled endlessly drawing water. Far in the distance, like mirages of floating clouds, were the mountains.

We bounced over the rutted track, seldom seeing signs of life, until suddenly around a turn we'd scatter small herds of goats or sheep. Once I saw a couple of stray camels nibbling at sparse naked trees. The heat, the dust, the smell seeped into the car and sapped every ounce of strength. The air was heavy and hard to breathe, liberally laced with the plume of apricot dust that trailed us. I was afraid I was going to be sick.

I closed my eyes and held my palm against my forehead, trying to block Elizabeth and Jai out of my mind. For three hours the bus followed the twisting, rising, meandering trail, stopping at intervals to leave packets of mail at small mud-walled villages filled with naked children, snarling pi-dogs, earth-colored people.

Again and again and again my mind would turn back to Elizabeth. *What have you done! In God's name, how can I help you—Elizabeth—Elizabeth!*

I was knotted into the corner of my seat, as oblivious to the miserable view as I could be, when the Sikh officer touched my arm and pointed out the window. "Kataipur," he said.

We had crested a steep rise. Below us were three lakes dotted with islands. One was covered with an elliptical temple, and far ahead was the village. It was crescent-shaped, wedged between a sparkling stream, the largest of the lakes, and a steeply-terraced hill.

Across the lake, outlining the shoulder of a sway-backed ridge, was a long, rose-colored crenellated wall, and at the apex were huge towers. I pointed and then asked my neighbor in Hindi, "And what is that?"

"The walls of Khilar Palace and Valhargath Fort."

"Oh." I stared at the massive ramparts silently—impressed, intimidated. How would I go about even gaining admission into such a fortress? If I saw Elizabeth, how could I help her? And if the Maharaja was as stubbornly set in the old ways as Singh had said, how could I—a woman—move against his built-in prejudices? If no one wanted me asking questions about Elizabeth, would they see to it that I disappeared also?

I broke out of my unpleasant reverie as the bus rattled down the horseshoe turns on two wheels and no brakes, bringing the mud-colored village into telescopic focus and curtaining off the lower lakes behind thick scallops of hills. We crossed a narrow bridge and almost immediately careened into a crossroads teeming with traffic. Our intrepid driver never slowed, and how the plodding donkeys, humpbacked oxen, loaded camels, squawking chickens, naked children, pi-dogs, and tongas kept from being run down I don't know. The sound of our horn was incessant, stopping only when the driver's thumb grew numb. Eventually he came to a halt in a street so narrow that the doors opened against a gray-white bull on one side and a bicycle tonga on the other. He turned around and announced proudly, for my benefit, "Kataipur Bus Station. Bye-bye, Memsahib," then got out quickly to open the door. He held up a dirt-crusted hand to assist me, and between them, the chauffeur and the Sikh, I negotiated the step and a widening, splattering puddle made by the bull.

The Sikh officer asked in Hindi if I needed a tonga and I nodded. "Yes, I'm going to the Moti Palace Hotel."

"It's not too far. *Koi hai*," he shouted to a tonga-wallah dozing in his carriage. "To the Moti Palace." He helped work my bags around the bull and the bus and into the tonga.

The hotel was on the outskirts of Kataipur and the tonga-wallah pedaled his way expertly through the crowded streets. Barbers were plying their trade on the walks, small pigeonhole shops displayed everything from saris and shoes to pots and pans, exactly as in every other village in India. Then the bustle of the town dropped behind us; we followed an uneven road that skirted a hill, coming at last to a side road. A small sign with an arrow pointing the way, printed in both Hindi and English, read *Moti Palace Hotel*. Huge iron-barred gates were pushed back on their hinges, and stone guardhouses on either side were empty. Here a broad double-laned road cut directly through extensive gardens to the palace.

As we neared the hotel I gripped the frame of the fringed canopy nervously. What was ahead for me? For me and Elizabeth?

chapter IV

The Moti Palace, traditional residence of the Yuvraj, the heir, of Kataipur, was a two-story, U-shaped, pink sandstone building trimmed in white marble. It looked rather like a peppermint ice-cream cake. We circled through a garden filled with deep shade, geometric patches of sun-bright lawn and herbaceous borders of blazing color. A pink and white striped awning arched over the drive in front of the flagged terrace that connected the wings. A doorman dressed in spotless white with a yellow cockade and royal crest on his turban welcomed me with a bow, his hands together, then helped me from the tonga. After the desert we'd come through, this looked like a bit of paradise.

I followed him into an oversized hall bracketed with curving staircases that led to each upstairs wing. Opposite were great teak doors, every inch covered with carving, which opened into an immense ballroom. Crystal chandeliers hung from ornate ceilings. Pastel Orientals woven to size, whose borders matched the wainscoting fretwork of traditional vines and lotus blossoms, covered most of the marble floors. Massive furniture of wood and cane with much ivory and mirror inlay was settled in the room with a heavy air of indestructible permanence. Velvet cushions, brocade table runners, elegant tapestries with caparisoned elephants and lion hunts showed its royal heritage.

But I also noticed that the chandeliers were dull with caked dust, the velvet cushions worn threadbare, the furniture scratched and marred with cigarette burns, and the exquisite rugs had ugly stains. No one who cared was taking care of the Moti Palace.

I registered in a small parlor lobby off the hall, then followed a red-turbaned bearer to my room. Long windows and french doors opened onto a balustraded balcony snuggled under an overgrown mulberry tree. The balcony overlooked the garden. On past I could see thin streams of smoke and the dun-colored roofs of a native compound. My eyes grew heavy in the bright light and I felt an overwhelming desire to sleep. As soon as the boy had gone, I pulled the slatted blinds and fell across the bed fully dressed. The soft whirring of the ceiling fan lulled me into a heavy sleep.

When I awoke it was dark, and I felt benumbed. I knew that I'd put myself to sleep as a sort of subconscious escape mechanism—I was afraid of what was before me. I sat up slowly, shook my head to clear it, and flicked on the light.

It was midnight. I pulled off my rumpled suit, took a cold shower, changed into blue jeans and a ribbed turtleneck sweater and walked to the window. I raised the blind and looked out over the garden. It was full of shadows; a pale quarter moon rolled on its back, barely lighting its spot of sky, and did nothing to dull the stars, low-hung and brilliant.

There was the constellation Orion the Hunter almost overhead, with those jewels Betelgeuse, his epaulet, and Rigel, the diamond buckle on his sandal, as familiar in this Indian sky as they were over University Lake. His Big Dog wore Sirius, the brightest star in the heavens, tagged at his throat. To the west was Taurus, his horns pointed menacingly at the Twins, Castor and Pollux, bravely holding hands. The stubborn Bull with his bright eye Aldebaran reminded me of Pita-Singh—and his Scorpio eyes. I shook my head. Why would I think of him now?

I pulled my thoughts back to the beautiful Indian night. There was a flutter in the mulberry tree as a restless bird changed perches. The luminous streak of the Milky Way in no wise dimmed the stars. The night was velvet-soft about me and the stars were pins that quilted it in place.

Out of sight to the front of the hotel would be the Great Bear with the Polaris Pointers racing the Dragon around the polestar. I breathed deep of the fragrant slow-moving breeze that barely ruffled the leaves of the mulberry tree.

Thoughts of Elizabeth came back like ever-rising cream to settle at the top of my mind. Certainly she was the victim of some terrible intrigue. First I would have to see her. Then—my imagination stopped. I had no idea how even to manage that.

Suddenly I was hungry. I couldn't remember when I'd eaten last. It must have been lunch in Darampur. More than likely there was no food service at this hour, but I'd find out.

In the hall, a sleepy room boy jumped to his feet as I closed the door. "Meesy? Meesy want?" I shook my head.

"Nothing now." I decided I'd rather approach the kitchen directly than to ask his help. I felt him staring after me perplexed as I went down the stairs. There was only the night clerk in the lobby, dozing in a wicker chair. I hated to bother him, and when I spoke he opened his eyes sleepily. "Do you suppose I could get a bite to eat, this late?" I asked.

"I'll see what I can find, Miss," he answered, smothering a yawn. "You'd like some fruit perhaps?"

"Anything would be fine." I walked across the veranda to the garden terrace, dimly lighted from the entry lanterns. It was deserted; chairs were tipped against the tables to shed the morning dew. Only a few lights showed in the hotel wing; the public rooms were dimmed. There was a sleepy chirp from a disturbed bird in a drooping acacia tree as I pulled back a chair and sat down. A tiger-striped cat slipped by silently on the prowl. There was the faint sound of the breeze through the mottled shadows and somewhere the tinkle of a wind chime. And far, far away so that it sounded like an echo of itself, I heard the jarring unmelodic sound of Indian music. That must be from the compound, I thought.

My room boy slipped up quietly to place a tray on the table. "Missy want something else, she call Mali, and I come running."

"Thank you, Mali. Now you go back to sleep." He nodded and grinned. I turned my full attention to the tray. There was cold rice, a banana, a chicken leg, chappatis, and a pot of tea. It tasted like a meal prepared in Heaven.

After I'd finished every crumb and only a swallow of tea remained, I fished a cigarette out of my pocket and was just ready to light it when a terribly familiar voice said, "May I?" And a lighter flamed in my face.

Bill Holmes! His seamless face was bland in the lamp-light and his pale eyes were almost colorless. He stood beside me with the flaming lighter, and if a completely characterless face could look grim, his did. But the surprising thing to me was how glad I was to see him. I held out my hands and he took them in his own thick soft ones. There was no feeling of recoiling I had always felt before when he touched me. Never would I have believed the day would come when I was frankly delighted to see Bill Holmes.

"Bill! I thought you were in Nepal—"

"I came back to welcome you. I thought you'd be here a couple of days ago. Are you sure you weren't drugged? You've been asleep for nine hours!"

"I know," I said, "I was dead."

"I've had your room boy looking in on you every hour and finally after I'd gone to bed, Menon, the room clerk, sent word that you were eating." He paused a minute and then bowed saying, "Welcome to Kataipur from a long-time resident of two days."

Then he sat down beside me, and I remembered the cigarette I was holding and let him light it. I looked at my watch. "It's a little late for a welcoming party. What are you doing here? I thought you were in Nepal getting a temple sculpture—"

"Sh-h-h!" he held his finger to his lips and rolled his eyes in an exaggerated gesture of conspiracy. "So the old man told you. He shouldn't have. The fewer who know about it, the safer the project is." He paused a minute, lighted his own cigarette and then added, "Especially right now—Bevan, Corraway is in trouble. He sent word to me in Katmandu. I hurried back here and talked to him." I waited expectantly; he was unaccountably serious. Moving his cigarette nervously around the brass ashtray until he'd worked its tip to a glowing point, he said suddenly, "Bevan, the damndest thing has happened." He crushed out his cigarette in a quick motion of temper.

"Well?"

"The sheriff's office served an injunction on him—"

"On Uncle Coe! Whatever for?"

"To restrain him from disposing of any part of the Sheridan Collection to the university."

"Bill, that's the most outrageous thing I've ever heard! Who did it?"

"The request came from Interpol. Evidently the Indian government instigated it—"

"Interpol! My God—somebody is really off base. You know as well as I that the Sheridan Collection is his personal property. He can damn well do what he wants with it!"

"Tell that to the Sheriff! Someone thinks that part of the collection was stolen and until they get those pieces back, all of it will be tied up."

"Bill, these trips you've been making—were they legitimate?"

"Of course! The stuff I've been bringing back has come from Nepal. All very legal. It's just when you're taking Indian artifacts out of the country that it gets sticky. They've gotten pretty unreasonable lately."

My cigarette had burned to my fingers unnoticed. I dropped it on the ground and crushed it. We stared at each other silently. This was the last thing I'd expected. "The university is really counting on the collection. I don't know what to say."

"I know. It really shook the old man."

I nodded, then looked away. The lamplight glowed against the leaves and turned them scarlet. I ran my tongue across my lips, wondering if I should tell him what I'd learned in Darampur, then decided I should. "I have some news, too, Bill. And it's all bad." I told him everything K. R. Singh had told me while I waited for the mail bus to Kataipur.

"Christ!" he said and that was all. We sat there under the acacia tree and the silence was all around us. Finally he asked, "Have you any plan?"

"Nothing, except I'm going to Khilar tomorrow and see what I can find."

"I'll go with you—"

"No," I shook my head. "I don't want you to. It's better for me to go alone. Have you heard anything since you've been here—anything about Elizabeth?"

"Not a thing. Of course, I haven't asked. I've been trying to clear my invoices. I don't want the news to filter out that I'm buying for Sheridan."

Clearly our minds were on different things and I had to make an effort to pull my thoughts back to his mission in Kataipur. "Do you already have the sculpture out of Nepal?"

"Yes, it's somewhere in the hills; it's coming overland across the mountains. Actually there's nothing to tie it to Sheridan."

"Good luck," I said. "I wish I could wrap up my mission as well."

"If there's any way I can help—"

"You can't—at least not now. I'll go to Khilar tomorrow and see if I can get my foot in the front door."

Bill stood up, reached for my hand, and patted it awkwardly. "Well, you've had your eight hours, but I haven't. I'm going to bed and I'll see you in the morning before you leave."

"Good night, Bill. I think I'll have another cigarette before I turn in." He brushed my cheek with a light kiss and crossed the terrace into the hotel. I lighted a cigarette and then followed him across the terrace to the veranda. I walked slowly, my hand lightly touching the damp coolness of the marble balustrade, fringes of bougainvillea brushing my hair, watching my shadow grow pale and lengthen as I moved away from the entry lamps. The air was heavy with the mixed fragrance of a score of night-blooming flowers. I leaned against a marble pillar and watched the thin stream of cigarette smoke disintegrate. The garden was dark, trees were silhouetted black against the sky. A night bird called softly and then was answered. Familiar stars in a familiar heaven clustered like shasta daisies over the fringe of trees. It was time to go in.

Then I heard the car. I watched as it turned into the hotel drive, its lights through the shrubbery growing larger until the whole entry was spotlighted. It stopped with a violent screeching of brakes. I moved farther into the shadow of the bougainvillea. There was no doorman, so the driver hopped out and held the car door open for his passenger.

I very nearly gasped aloud. My hand flew to my mouth in unfeigned surprise, and I stood there frozen while the man I'd said good-bye to at the Washington airport climbed out of the car, ran up the steps, and crossed the veranda into the hotel, followed by the taxi driver who brought his suitcase, briefcase, and trench coat. It is certainly one small world, I thought. I stayed on the veranda long afterward, wondering who he was and what he was doing *here?*

In the lobby I stopped to ask the clerk, "The man who just came in—I think I know him—"

"Shri Vehta, miss. He lives here. He just arrived from the States."

Confused, I shook my head. "No, I don't suppose I

know the gentleman after all. The name doesn't mean anything. . . ." But it did. It was a stupefying bit of knowledge. Elizabeth was married to a Vehta. Was this man a brother? This—this Pita-Singh? No, of course not. They—they were all dead. Then who could he be? I asked, "Is there a train this time of night?"

"Yes. It was late, just arriving from Darampur. I hope the Memsahib Doctor enjoyed her dinner."

"I did." And I smiled at the sleepy clerk. "It was delicious and I thank you so much—"

"Also Shri Holmes has been waiting all day—so anxious to see you—"

"Yes, I know. An old friend."

"Ah, yes. An old friend of mine also."

I looked at him curiously. What did he mean by that? Or was he just making conversation, waiting for me to leave and go back to my room? All the way up the stairs my mind whirled. The Hindu, Pita-Singh, lived here! And if it hadn't been for the Sikh taxi driver we would have arrived together on the same train. But why had the room clerk not called him Pita-Singh. I stopped quickly and gripped the marble bannister. Jai Vehta was the man Elizabeth married. They had to be some kin. What had this man been doing at the university, besides wanting my Deccan *Katar* and threatening Mr. Sheridan's collection? *Then I understood.* He was the man who had caused the injunction to be served on the collection. He was also the man who had threatened Bill Holmes. I wondered if he knew Bill was here now? Did he know I was?

It took a pill to get me to sleep, and when I awakened the sun was high. A rhythmic pounding came through the window from far away, and I lay there several minutes trying to place the sound. It was low and muffled by distance, as steady as a hundred heartbeats. Finally I opened the blinds. It didn't come from the native compound. I stood there listening, curious. A whirl of pigeons swarmed by to rest in the mulberry tree. The purple bougainvillea that had draped itself on the roof over the balcony gave the room a lavender cast. Then I remembered what I had to do and dressed quickly.

I wondered if Bill had eaten. I was more than a little relieved when I saw the night clerk was gone and a new man was there.

"Pardon, please," I said, "but will you ring Shri Vehta?"

He smiled and shook his head. "I'm sorry, Memsahib, but Shri Vehta left an hour or so ago for Khilar Palace. Was he expecting you to call?"

"Oh, no. It isn't important. I'll be going to the palace today. But thank you. Is Mr. Holmes down?"

"On the veranda, Mem, having breakfast."

I had tea and rolls while Bill sat opposite me in a wicker chair and smoked. And although we sat there together for some time, I didn't tell him about the Indian named Shri Vehta who had come directly from Midwestern University to Kataipur. And for the life of me I didn't know why. We discussed my plans for breaching the palace and wondered if I'd have any trouble getting in. If Elizabeth was there—what then? Suppose she wasn't, would they tell me where to find her? What if she—No! Of course she was alive! I mustn't think along such lines. Certainly I would see her.

Back in my room I dressed carefully. I put on a beige cotton suit with a white blouse and my string of coral beads. I wore white gloves and pulled my hair back with a flat white bow at the nape of my neck. I put aside my shoulder bag in preference to a brown envelope purse and then I added my horn-rimmed sun glasses. When I saw my reflection I looked fifteen years older; or, I thought, mocking the serious face that stared back at me, perhaps I looked my age. The desk clerk eyed me curiously when I asked him to call a taxi.

"There's only one, Dr. Blakley, but he should be back soon. Where do you want to go?"

"To Khilar Palace. Since it's such a great distance, do you suppose the driver could wait for me?"

"No, Memsahib, he can't do that. He has to meet the plane this afternoon; today it comes from Calcutta. But they will call one for you from the palace."

Bill waited with me on the veranda until a rickety cab wheezed up the drive. The white-turbaned doorman explained to the driver that I wanted to go to the palace and then he helped me in with such deference that I concluded a taxi ride to the palace rated immediate status. I waved to Bill and he made a circle with his thumb and forefinger wishing me luck.

Near the village the chauffeur, in contrast to the driver of the mail car, wove his way carefully through a jumbled crowd that was coming and going. In the heart of the town we slowed to a snail's pace, stopping often when the street was blocked by the busy clutter of life.

As we worked our way through the village I got occasional glimpses of the lake at the ends of narrow alleys, and once a quick view of the river cascading through the water gate. Women stood knee deep in the water, pounding their clothes. That was the thudding beat I had heard. Soon we left the last of the brown huts behind us and the road turned abruptly, so that the lake, a lovely cornflower blue, was on one side, and on the other steeply-terraced hills reached upward as far as I could see. The road was deserted, in marked contrast to the one on the other side of the village. We met only a few farmers bringing produce to market, and they moved off the road with a resigned submission as we neared. I wondered if they hadn't been doing just that for hundreds of years when any vehicle approached on the road to Khilar Palace.

The lake, marbled with ripples from the water gate, reached to the horizon rim where an encircling arm of lavender hills dissolved into insubstantial whiffs of clouds. There were occasional fishermen's boats, small brown-sailed skiffs whose design hadn't changed in a thousand years.

On the far hill-ridge was the rose-colored rampart that ambled above the lake and was reflected in it, reminding me of pictures I'd seen of the great Chinese Wall, and at its farthest tip was the silhouette of the old buttressed fort and its towers. The midday sun shimmered off the lake and flashed sharply from marble domes barely visible inside the wall. In minutes the road edged away to loop in easy turns into the hills. High on the outside curves I could see the other lakes, each dropping lower than the first, connected with dams and overflow waterfalls. They dipped away from the hills like a sapphire lavalier. Each seemed smaller than the preceding one, and I wondered if they really were, or if it was simply the perspective. They were speckled with dots of islands like tiny brown toads playing leapfrog, with the temple island dominating them all. Rising out of the lake like a mirage the temple entirely covered the island that supported it. It had one enormous football-shaped tower with smaller, identical ones clustered like warped mushrooms around it.

Then we lost the lakes altogether and hairpinned down into a broad valley as desolate and arid as the land beyond Kataipur. It was several miles further before we approached the wall and I was surprised at the size of it

—its height and breadth. The taxi slowed behind a bullock cart and I looked out the rear window. The view from this distance was breathtaking. The scimitar-shaped village was wrapped around the top curve of the lake. The cluster of flat, dirt-colored rooftops was interspersed with occasional clumps of dark trees. On the near bank a diamond-studded river showed itself briefly before it disappeared into the furrowed hills behind the town.

Sitting there in the ramshackle taxi I remembered back to that day at the university when Elizabeth had sat in my office at the museum and told me the history of the family. And from that day to this moment I hadn't thought of it. Now it loomed like a dark shadow rising from my memory.

Jai's ancestors, linked to the solar dynasty through Lava, one of the twin sons of Lord Rama, founded the kingdom of Kataipur eight centuries ago in this secluded valley of the Himalayan foothills. The tide of Islam had swept over them and around them, leaving little influence except on the architecture of the palace so that it glittered with breast-shaped domes with jeweled nipples. Bending like reeds, giving a little—but never all—hedging here and there, taking one step forward and only half a step backward, keeping as their motto *No step forward is ever lost,* the family had survived through the centuries, exacting loyalty and taxes from the villagers.

In return the family had furnished protection from bandits who preyed on the caravans bringing salt from the west and furs and silks from the east, and assisted pilgrims who trekked to the source of the Ganges. The Muslims and the Hindus settled down then to live in comparative peace with only occasional feuds with their neighboring states until the Portuguese came, and after them the French and the British. In the end there were only the

British. The Indians made one last effort at independence —the Sepoy Rebellion—then the family was united by treaty to the British Raj.

After freedom, the Maharaja exchanged several hundred acres of land to the government for a tax-free stipend, the privy purse, which had just now been reneged. But by any odds the Maharaja and his family were fantastically wealthy. The symbol of their power was a jewel- and gold-encrusted ivory throne that dated from the thirteenth century—and I could almost see the despotic Maharaja in his robes and turban sitting squarely upon it, dispensing justice. Was that the way it happened to Elizabeth?

I rolled down my window and the noises from the palace compound poured through the car in a cacophony of sounds. There was the plaintive bleating of a goat tied to a dust-choked tree beside the trefoil gate. There were shouting vendors laden with everything from pots and pans to betel nuts and water jugs. And from everywhere was the earthy odor of animals and humans. The heat-saturated walls of the Khilar Palace ramparts beat down upon me like a tangible spirit of this land. But it was more than a spirit—it was an emotion—and with it came tension. This was the palace Elizabeth knew. Where she lived, where she had loved Jai.

The cart moved through the center of the multi-storied gate and we followed it into the compound. A few neem trees were anchored into eroded, cement-hard ground showing great naked roots, snaking this way and that. Children played around bicycles, carts, and tongas that were parked haphazardly beneath them. Native men squatted on their haunches in clustered groups smoking, dozing, or playing cards on string beds.

Tattered little stalls covered with dun-colored canvas or corrugated tin roofs filled with earthenware jars and fruits and vegetables and merchandise jutted out irregularly along the inside wall as far as I could see.

Everything was wilted by the noonday heat. Shadows were short and only the children moved quickly, noisily. We drove down the center road carefully while those few natives who were about moved slowly and deliberately out of our way. A quarter of a mile further we passed through an arched gateway in the stone walls, bracketed by immense iron gates which stood open, and entered a cobbled courtyard that reflected the heat like the inside of an oven. A drift of trees edged the far side of the yard where a belled and tasselled horse jingled as he flicked his tail, and a few turbaned, dhoti-clad men played cards on a charpoy. A massive fountain formed of carved lotus leaves and blossoms stood in the center of the courtyard but was dry and didn't appear to have had any water in the last hundred years.

The palace itself was a fantastic structure stretching—how far? A quarter of a mile, half a mile, a mile? I had no idea. It was longer than any building had a right to be. At the far end it was connected to the ancient ruins of the fort. A marble walkway bracketed with a double line of great sandstone elephants, each carrying a lotus in its trunk and a howdah on its caparisoned back, led directly to the palace. Two uniformed guards stood at attention beneath white-fringed yellow umbrellas on either side of the steps. In their crested turbans they seemed seven feet tall, and I knew they were part of the Maharaja's private constabulary. They looked neither to the right nor the left and seemed impervious to the heat. My driver stopped at the elephant walk.

I asked him if he'd wait, but he shook his head. "Airplane from Calcutta—come now." As soon as I paid and tipped him, he flashed a white-toothed grin and climbed back in his car. He waved as he drove away, and I wondered if he had any idea how truly alone and small I felt standing there between the massive stone elephants.

I looked up at the weathered rose-colored walls which absorbed the sun and seemed to tame it, dwarfing everything below. Hundreds of purdah windows looked back at me and behind the fretworked patterns I imagined invisible eyes, more than could be counted, staring at me. In hate? In curiosity? In hope? Were they real or were they ghosts? Was Elizabeth there looking down at me?

At each corner of this square section of the palace were sugar-frosted cupolas topped with faceted crystal which reflected light like giant diamonds. I glanced around the courtyard, feeling its noonday lethargy, then took a deep bolstering breath of the heavy air saturated with ten thousand smells. I walked up the marble path between the elephants, past the stolid guards and up the stairs, hollowed by centuries of sandaled feet. At their top was a broad mosaic terrace and in front of me were triple pairs of massive bronze doors twenty feet high. I wondered if I should knock, and if so where?

The center doors opened; someone had been watching. I was bowed into the palace by a black-eyed butler in white with a yellow turban bearing a gold-embroidered crest and a matching sash that nipped in the waist of his knee-length jacket. I felt a small degree of triumph.

Inside it was marvelously cool. I was in a huge entrance hall, its floor and walls of marble inlaid with every color and kind of semiprecious stones which made patterns of lotus blossoms and trailing vines and jungle animals and peacocks and parrots. Moorish arches laced with marble filigree led to other corridors that seemed to fan out in all directions. A fountain splashed in the center of the room and fell back into a quatrefoil basin sunk in the floor that held a dozen or more goldfish, whose gossamer fins fluttered like Salome's seven veils. There was little furniture, only low benches cushioned in faded brocades lined the walls between the corridors.

A balcony hidden with stylized fretwork was opposite the entry, and I wondered how many generations of concubines or wives had watched receptions in the giant hall, seeing but unseen. Below the balcony was a corridor several times as wide as the others that led directly to a garden. Beyond, I could see, as if looking through the wrong end of a telescope, a bit of the lake.

The bearer left and I wondered who would come to meet me. After a minute or two of waiting, I crossed the hall to the opposite corridor. My heels clicked like castanets at each step. Floors such as these were made to be walked on with velvet slippers. Then suddenly I felt rather than heard the presence behind me and turned.

He was a rather small man with broad shoulders, dressed in white jodhpurs and a Nehru jacket that emphasized the brightness of his eyes and shiny brown skin. His hair and eyebrows were almost the same color as his complexion. His eyes watched me, rather, I imagined, as a tiger might. They were black beads that clung to drooping lids which cut them almost in half; a startling white crescent showed beneath. He held his hands behind him.

"Madame, whom do you wish to see?" There was civil politeness in each syllable of his excellent English that was typically Indian in its inflection and rhythm. Crisply correct, proper, with just the right amount of condescension, I felt his hostility instantly.

I stood my ground and answered with a false, defiant courage, "Will you please notify Madame Elizabeth Vehta that Dr. Bevan Blakley from Midwestern University is here to see her." I stared him down. His eyes shifted suddenly and he looked past me into the garden before he answered. "Madame Vehta is not at the palace presently. I'm extremely sorry that you have undertaken such a long journey in vain. When I see Madame I shall tell her you called. Good day." He turned and walked to the door, expecting me to follow. Instead I went the other direction to the garden. A terrace bordered the garden on three sides. It was shaded by an overhanging balcony scalloped with vines, and there were pleasant groupings of wicker furniture with faded cretonne cushions and low tables beside them. The north side was open spectacularly to the lake. Short noontime shadows of palm, mango, and neem trees fell across curlicued patches of lawn and flowerbeds. Through it all was a maze of flagstoned paths. A large fountain spewed crystal jets of water in the air and overflowed its basin, making a circular waterfall that splashed into an oblong lotus pond filled with golden carp.

There were thousands of flowers—marigolds, salvia, nasturtiums, poinsettias, bougainvillea, red and pink and white. A convolvulus creeper of heady blue morning glories as large as my hand hung thick from a bamboo trellis and next to that was a white drapery of jasmine. I broke off a branch and twisted it in my hands. Then suddenly I knew there was something wrong. All these flowers—and there was no fragrance; all these flowers and not a bee. These thick-leaved trees and not a sign of a bird, not a sound even from an unseen one. All the garden was smothered in a deathlike stillness. There was not even the chirp of a cricket, not a butterfly, not an insect. Only an unnerving, disquieting silence.

The sky was seared to an anemic blue by the midday sun, but here was a lovely fairy-tale land that spoke of death. An acrid decaying odor of humus, a stagnant, bitter death's-head dust permeated the garden. A clutching fear, a growing horror enveloped me and I longed to cry *Elizabeth—Elizabeth, come with me—escape!*

Two tiers of balconies, their balustrades dripping with red bougainvillea, their moorish arches fringed with vines, rimmed the garden. I looked at them frantically, searching, praying that I could see Elizabeth; willing her to hear my thought. *Elizabeth, Elizabeth, answer me—call to me!* But there was no sign she was near.

"Since the one you came to see is unavailable, is there someone else?" the man asked, suddenly appearing at my side.

"The Maharaja?" I suggested boldly.

"The Maharaja, Madame, sees no one."

"Then I'll see Mr. Vehta." His expression changed and there was a flicker of surprise in his eyes. Then instantly he had control of himself and said, "Shri Vehta was here this morning. But he left. I do regret, Madame, that your long trip has accomplished nothing. I have called the car for you."

"I'm not going," I answered evenly. "Not until I see someone in authority who will tell me about Elizabeth Vehta."

"I am the authority, and all I can tell you is that Madame Vehta is not at Khilar Palace."

"Then where *is* she?" I asked between clenched teeth.

"She is in custody," he answered calmly, his eyes as unblinking as a statue.

So it was true. I hoped that the dismay I felt wasn't reflected in my face. "Why is that?" I persisted stubbornly.

"The American daughter-in-law of the Maharaja has been tried and sentenced according to Kataipur law for the murder of her husband. Now I need to return to His Highness. There is nothing further I can tell you—"

"I'll go to the American consul—to the American ambassador—"

"Madame, it has been investigated by your government, and in matters of criminal proceedings an alien is subject to the laws of India. You are certainly welcome to do any investigating you'd like. But I can tell you this—Madame Elizabeth Vehta confessed to the murder of her husband, which in itself was enough to destroy the old Maharaja. I will see you to the car."

I didn't answer. There was nothing to say. It was as if my mind and body were paralyzed by the information he'd given me. I stood there on the marble terrace looking across the lovely garden that smelled of death, to the pale lake as smooth as any mirror, and on to the amethyst hills. I could do nothing. Oh! Elizabeth—Elizabeth. Somewhere from far away I heard him say again, "Madame, the car is waiting." Then I saw a movement, as infinitesimal as the flicker of an eyelid, and I watched a cobra slither out from the shadow of the lotus pond. It came straight toward me and, paralyzed, I didn't move. Before it reached the terrace, it lifted itself higher and higher, swaying, much like a reed in a breeze, its jet-bead eyes staring at me, its gold-brown hood flared, its eye-like markings swaying with a hypnotic rhythm, and I stood entranced, immobile, scarcely breathing.

I knew, of course, that the king cobra—Naja-Naja—was sacred to many Hindus. He is a living fertility symbol, the lingam of Vishnu, and is worshipped by women all over India who prostrate themselves within striking distance of dozens during the serpent festival of Naga Panchami. Indian literature is filled with stories of cobras shielding kings and heroes and the god Krishna from the sun by spreading their hoods above them. I knew all this—but I wasn't a believer. I dared not take my eyes off him to look at the man beside me. Even as I stared at the cobra, it dropped to the ground and inched to a saucer of milk I hadn't noticed before and drank. And I knew how Elizabeth's young nephew had died. I knew, as well as if it had been written on the back of his flared hood, that this was the cobra who struck the child.

I could go now. The snake had put things back into perspective for me.

There was nothing more I could do. I was out of my element here—and the man beside me knew it. I glanced at him as I turned and saw a gleam of satisfaction in his eyes. He had defeated me, and I felt a dreadful loneliness for Elizabeth. I had no chance to see her. There was no way, no way at all. I walked to the entrance where the turbaned butler stood inside the open doors.

The car, a Rolls-Royce of ancient vintage, waited near the elephant path, and I walked to it slowly. A bearded chauffeur I recognized as a Sikh, and who wore a white turban with the same gold crest as the bearer, held the door for me. This would be K. R. Singh's brother. I didn't look back.

Before I reached the car I noticed the holy man. He was sitting on a small earthen mound covered with reed matting beneath a large peepul tree—the holy tree of India, a giant fig. It wasn't far from the palace gate and I wondered that I hadn't noticed him when I arrived. The sadhu was shriveled and bony, his naked body was smeared with ashes, his gray hair matted to his shoulders. He sat cross-legged as holy men have ever sat in dictate to Krishna's directions in the *Bhagavad-Gita*—body, neck and head straight and still, every muscle controlled in deepest meditation, eyes disciplined. But the old sadhu's eyes weren't staring at the root of his nose as Krishna had directed. They stared at me, red-rimmed, pale, feverish, from the folds of his ancient face that was as brown and wrinkled as a walnut. He held me in his gaze so firmly that it took a physical effort to break away and move to the car. Then I stopped.

"One minute," I said to the driver. I walked to the sadhu. A small group of men stood to one side and they moved back as I approached. *"Panditji,"* I whispered in Hindi, "I have need of your blessing." I laid the branch of jasmine I'd carried from the garden beside him on the reed matting, then impulsively I pulled the coral necklace over my head and placed it in his begging bowl. I curtsied with my head bowed and my palms together and whispered, *"Namaste."* I didn't wait for an answer. I didn't expect one. The Sikh driver eyed me curiously as he closed the door. But I looked past him, past the statue-like guards, through the iron gates to the village compound. Putting on my glasses, I slipped into a sort of gray-colored anonymity behind them.

We drove through the gates into the endless street filled with people, and my mind orbited around Elizabeth. Was she alive? How did I know? Why hadn't the State Department contacted her aunt? Perhaps Elizabeth didn't want them to. Now it was too late. Even I realized that. Officials would be more interested in keeping a diplomatic status quo than seeing to justice. But—I rationalized my thinking—that isn't so. Elizabeth had confessed to killing her husband. Was it under torture? Or had she simply been goaded into a situation in which she wanted to kill him—a temporary insanity. I should have asked. There is certainly a legal difference between premeditated murder and the sudden passion of anger. Except perhaps in such developing countries where women have no rights. Surely she'd had a lawyer. Why hadn't I thought to get his name? I simply had not used my head.

So my thoughts went, leapfrogging from one thing to another during the ride back through the hills, along the lake, the creeping progress through the town, until we reached the Moti Palace. The hotel seemed an almost blessed haven after Khilar and I climbed out of the car quickly before the doorman could open it. I had neither thanks nor a backward glance for the driver. He was the Sikh's brother—but he also knew where Elizabeth was. He'd probably taken her there in this ancient Rolls.

chapter V

Bill was in the bar when I returned. I sat down beside him and ordered a lemonade. "It must have been rugged if it put you on the wagon," he commented dryly.

I sighed. "It was simply ghastly. Elizabeth's in prison somewhere—and, Bill, she confessed to killing Jai."

Bill didn't answer for some time. He twisted his glass on the bar and the muscle in his jaw tightened. "God!" he whispered half under his breath. "What can you do?"

"Nothing—really. Even the State Department has given up on her. I don't know why Miss Edith wasn't told about it. Maybe Elizabeth didn't want her to know."

"Who did you talk to?"

"I don't know. The majordomo, the curator, the librarian, clerk of the works. . . . Hell, Bill, he gave me the runaround all the way and showed me to the door. On top of that—there was a cobra."

He looked at me, startled. "A cobra!"

"A family pet. They keep a saucer of milk for him—"

"The only thing I can say is you'd better put some vodka in that lemonade." He offered me a cigarette and then lighted it.

"No." I shook my head and let a stream of smoke filter slowly through my lips. "I have too much deep and serious thinking to do. And when I'm thinking seriously and deeply, like right now, I'm not a drinking woman." I tried to make my tone light and I even managed a smile, but I knew it was a sick one from Bill's expression.

"Then I'll drink for both of us. If I can help you, Bevan—" I reached over and took his hand. For the first time in my life I was glad to have him around.

"Bill, just having you here is more help than you know." I gathered up my purse, slipped off the bar stool, then kissed him on the cheek, which surprised us both. "I'm going to get a bite to eat and take a nap. Dinner at eight?"

"Righto, as us British chaps say. And a bit of a drink at sevenish?" He did sometimes act giddy.

"Okay." Bill needed to be taken in small doses.

I had a hard time choking down the lunch that was brought to my room and a nap was out of the question. There was no way I could tame the wild succession of thoughts pouring through my mind so that I could rest. Finally I took a pen and stationery pad to the veranda and began a letter to Lane Thomas. Perhaps if I could get everything down on paper, my own thoughts would be more manageable. And besides, he would have to be the one to tell Miss Edith about Elizabeth. I simply couldn't write to her that her niece had been tried and sentenced to prison for a murder she'd confessed to—the murder of her husband.

I asked about Bill when I came down, but the clerk said only that he wasn't in the hotel and, although I was curious, it soon slipped from my mind and I concentrated on my letter to Lane. I had just finished it and was sealing the flap of the envelope when I saw a small boy creeping through the garden, deliberately staying out of sight of the doorman. Intrigued, I watched his progress from bush to bush and tree to tree until he disappeared from sight altogether. I wondered what the scrubby youngster was up to, then was surprised when his head popped up in front of me and two large brown eyes peered at me through the spindles of the balustrade.

"Memsab—Meesi—Memsab. . . ." I started to get up, but he shook his head quickly, put his finger to his lips, then shifted his eyes to where the doorman stood, and then back to me. So I sat quietly watching as he slipped a note onto the veranda, weighted it with a fair-sized pebble, then slipped away as silently as he'd appeared.

I glanced toward the doorman, Jamad, who stood stiffly erect looking down the driveway. Rising, I picked up the soiled slip of paper and unfolded it. "Twelve this night where the Jamshed Road meets Moti Ghat." It was printed crudely, unevenly, and there was no signature.

I ran my tongue across my lower lip and then chewed on it until suddenly I realized it hurt. Certainly I hadn't expected anything like this when I gave the sadhu the jasmine and my coral necklace—because, of course, it was from the holy man. It had to be—unless it was a trap from the palace majordomo to get rid of me. And that would be rather dangerous, for both of us. No, it had to be from the sadhu—he was going to help me find Elizabeth. I shoved the note into the pocket of my jacket, then walked down the steps, nodded to the bearer and followed the driveway to the Kataipur road. There was no one on it except an old peasant and a donkey burdened with wood. No small boy was anywhere in sight.

I reread the note, then folded it carefully into a small square which I smoothed with my fingers, ironing out the wrinkles as I walked back to the hotel. "Jamad," I asked, "where is the Moti Ghat?"

"It is the washing ghat, Memsahib. Where the river flows into the lake at the water gate. The laundry boys and the old women go there to beat their clothes on the steps. You can hear them early every morning; the slap-slap echoes through the village and across the lake." I knew. I'd heard them that morning.

"Is it far? Too far to walk?"

He shrugged. "Two—kilometre—three perhaps."

"And how would I find it if I walked alone?"

"The road to the village, you know it?"

I nodded. "Yes."

"You follow the road to the village, then at the temple go through the courtyard and you'll see the lake. You walk straight there and you'll find the washing ghat, called Moti —the Pearl."

"And the Jamshed Road?"

He looked at me and a strange expression crossed his face. At first I thought he wasn't going to answer and then he shrugged a little and said, "The Jamshed Road you will see as you leave the temple compound. It is the first road to the right—it curves down to the water gate steps. But Memsahib, I don't think—that is to say I wouldn't. . . ." His mumbling confusion trailed off to an unspoken thought when a horse tonga came trotting up the drive with Bill.

Bill paid the driver and said, "The only way to travel in India. At least the pedestrians let you by." He climbed out and added, "You look beautifully rested. Have you done enough serious thinking so that you can imbibe a wee cocktail?"

"Absolutely." I tapped the letter against my hand. "I wrote it all down, as the headshrinkers say, and now my burden is heaped on the broad shoulders of Lane Thomas. May the Lord preserve him!" We walked into the lobby together. I left the letter at the desk to be mailed, then followed Bill into the bar. We talked about prudent, noncommittal things, both of us deliberately staying away from those affairs uppermost in our minds. And still I didn't tell Bill about Shri Vehta Pita-Singh, and I didn't tell him about the old sadhu and the note he'd sent. He might insist on going with me. When I went upstairs to change, I knew that it wouldn't be easy slipping out immediately after dinner. Bill would wonder. And I needed to give myself plenty of time to get there—even allow some time in case I got lost.

I was preoccupied at dinner and so was Bill. Our conversation lagged. My mind was solely on the midnight tryst I was to keep with a poor bony old sadhu who would help me find Elizabeth. I excused myself as soon as I could after coffee. Bill said he was turning in, too. "I'm tired. See you in the morning—early?"

"Not too early," I answered. "Away from school I'm a ten o'clock scholar."

"Right. Good night, Bevan."

Back in my room, I undressed quickly and changed to jeans and a dark blue shirt. I wondered if tennis sneakers would show up too much at night but, remembering the dusty road to the village, I knew they'd not be white long. I left my purse and passport, but folded some rupee notes into a hip pocket. I needed to leave the hotel without being seen. I looked out the balcony at the mulberry tree—would it be possible?

It was. I shinnied down the tree as if I'd been doing such acrobatics all my life, and received only a scratched elbow. I breathed a quick prayer that I'd not be detected and crossed the garden to the far end of the drive, keeping the shrubbery between me and the veranda where I could hear guests laughing and chairs scraping. Just as I reached the Kataipur road a car turned in the drive, and I slipped into the shadow of a tree. It was the same limousine that had brought me from the Khilar Palace and as it passed the dim light that marked the entrance of the Moti Palace drive, I recognized Shri Vehta. He seemed to look straight at me and almost immediately the car slowed to a stop. I moved further into the shrubbery and dropped to the ground. I heard the car door slam and could see the long beams that spotlighted the road toward the Moti Palace. Then I heard them, the two men. They were speaking English. "I suppose it's foolish, but I thought I saw someone I know. . . ." His clipped British accent was easy to identify.

"But, Highness, in these bushes?"

"Yes, damn it, in these bloody bushes!" They passed within a few feet of me, then walked back to the car. "It's all right, Pandu, we'll go now."

"Highness is satisfied?" There was a question there that stated very clearly that if His Highness was satisfied, he wasn't. Was His Highness losing his mind? At least I didn't hear Shri Vehta answer and I let my breath out slowly. I heard the car engine start and watched the headlights move up the drive. Only then did I creep out of my hiding place and take the road to the village.

The same moon, a fraction heavier than the night before, rested on silver-brushed clouds. The same stars were thick and low. It was abnormally quiet. No wind even to rustle the leaves. Shri Vehta—the driver had called him Highness. I had a full curiosity about the man.

Occasionally I'd disturb a bird as I walked and it

would chatter softly, but all about me was a soft and smothering stillness. My tennis shoes left no sound along the dusty track.

It took the better part of an hour to reach the temple. Bodies swathed in white that made them glow like phosphorescent mummies were inside the walled courtyard, asleep in corners, curled up by the stairs, or stretched out comfortably on the still-warm paving. I stepped over them gingerly and had the eerie feeling of walking through a city of the dead until I passed the opposite gate and, after a false turn or two, found the Jamshed Road.

It was a narrow curving lane, dark from the shadows of houses. A few upper windows were lighted. Only men were about. As they passed, I'd slip into a recessed door. Once I heard the sound of angry voices and a girl child's sharp cry, then the solid thud of someone falling. I swallowed hard and hurried on. From somewhere a radio blasted out the wailing tones of Indian music. Surely it couldn't be much further. Was I lost? Would the old sadhu be there waiting for me, sitting on his reed matting beside the lake?

Suddenly I saw the glimmer of the lake in front of me, a small spot of star-splashed water, and I hurried toward it. I thought I heard the rush of footsteps behind me, but took no notice. The broad steps were there where the river poured over them into the lake, and I knew that I'd reached the Pearl Ghat called Moti—the same as the palace.

Here also was a narrow alley opening onto Jamshed Road. Looking down I could see shuttered windows from which narrow cracks of light showed. Here, too, was discordant, undulating music seeping through heavy doors, and shrill cries and coarse laughter. I paused when I saw two men standing there, then turned to go to the water gate. One of the men stepped in front of me.

"Memsahib, what you seek is here. . . ." His voice was low, blurred with a marked accent I couldn't place so that I barely understood him. In the darkness I couldn't see their faces, only the dull white of their jackets and turbans. Their feet were bare beneath tattered jodhpur pants, and I noticed that in spite of the noise from the alley, there was no one else around. "You come," the other man said as he too stepped in front of me. "You come now." He took my arm to propel me down the alley.

A twist of fear curled through me and I held back. "No," I whispered, shaking my head. "I seek the holy man."

"Memsahib, you come now. We take you—" His voice was low but stridently insistent. Something stopped me. I suddenly realized, with paralyzing fear, the danger I had allowed myself to fall into—alone in the dark alley with two men whose faces I couldn't see. I shook my head and pulled away from them into Jamshed Road.

Then suddenly one pushed a cloth into my face, and I recognized the strong odor of chloroform. I tried to scream and couldn't. A stupefying terror surged through me, turning my legs to rubber. I stumbled against the stone building. Unseen hands were snatching at me, pulling me. . . .

I heard a shout and a curse. I fell to the street, free of the rag that had smothered me. The cobblestone paving was cool and damp. I was breathing again. No one held me—I was free, but too weak to get up. Then I was conscious of the sound of shattering, pulverizing blows, stunned grunts of pain, the slap of running feet. I realized that there was someone with me and he was lifting me to my feet, trying to brace my liquid legs—that his arms were strong and warm. Through the cloudy din that was ringing in my ears I heard his voice and recognized it. "My dear Dr. Blakley, I do find you in the damndest places. What in the name of God are you doing here?"

"Well, it's none of your business—" My legs were suddenly stiff, and if I was glad to see Mr. Highness Vehta, I wasn't going to show it. I took a long breath and expelled it with a shaky laugh. "What do you suppose they wanted?"

"You mean you walk alone through an alley like this and when you're accosted you don't know why? You must be simple or stupid—and somehow I'd never thought of you as either."

I jerked away from him angrily. "You don't understand. I had an appointment—"

"In the alley of prostitutes called Jamshed Road? Dr. Blakley, please—I'm not that naïve."

"I didn't know. . . ." My voice trailed off as I realized that I had been incredibly gullible. How could I tell this man that I asked an ash-smeared sadhu for help and thought it had come. To believe in miracles—Yes, I was both simple and stupid, but I'd never under God's heaven admit it—not to this self-righteous man with his sticky British accent.

I knew now, of course, that the old holy man had nothing to do with the note I'd received. He was inherently good; I'd felt it. Those men—those men who accosted me were purely evil. Had they been among those near the sadhu in the courtyard and heard my whispered plea for help? Or had they—and my breath caught—come from the palace? A simple way to get rid of a curious, stupid woman? I'd never know. What if this overbearing man hadn't come?

I knew one thing—I'd never tell him I had come to Jamshed Road seeking news of Elizabeth.

I pushed the hair away from my face and turned back the way I'd come, the tall Hindu beside me, in a silence that was about to explode. Finally he said, "Times must really be hard nowadays in the brothels along Jamshed Alley." I couldn't help but shiver, and he continued, "They're usually looking for luscious ripe maidens of thirteen to sixteen. You're a little old for the average Moslem's taste. But then as I say, times are difficult—"

"Go to Hell!" I said.

Then, as though talking to himself, he continued, "Couldn't believe my eyes. To see someone I thought I'd left in the States backed up against a bloody palm tree in the Moti Palace garden was more than passing strange. But when Pandu and I saw you huddled like a little bunny in the bushes, I was plain damn curious to know what you were up to. I sent him to the hotel and I followed you."

My anger melted away as quickly as it had flared. I stopped and touched his arm. "Believe me, I'm not ungrateful—"

He shrugged. "That's all right. I learned long ago to return good for evil, to cast bread on the waters. Everything in your Christian philosophy has been proved in our short, unstable acquaintance."

"All right," I said, and somehow seemed short of breath. The long walk, of course—and the traumatic incident of almost being kidnapped and thrown into a Moslem brothel. God knows that would be enough to leave any girl breathless. Then I added, "I understand, perhaps, although I'll admit nothing, about the evil and the good, but the bread—I can't see it ever returning."

"Ah," he said vaguely, "you will. . . ." He looked down at my hand on his arm and then our eyes locked in the moonlight by the temple gate and couldn't turn loose. My fingers seemed to have caught fire and I dropped my hand quickly and forced my eyes away. I felt his nearness and couldn't understand my confusion. There were a million things I wanted to ask him.

We walked through the temple courtyard and on to the Moti Palace road, occasionally brushing shoulders, arms, hands. And I felt a quick sensitive warmth when they touched. We walked in silence. There didn't seem to be any need for talk.

At the hotel, when we reached the veranda, I asked suddenly, "Who . . . who are you?"

"Park, my English friends call me. Prakash Pita-Singh Vehta—that's one of the Kshatriya, the warrior caste. Pita-Singh—that's because Akbar thought an ancient ancestor fought so valiantly against him he dubbed him 'Brave and Splendid Father of a Lion.' We dropped the 'brave and splendid' because they seemed redundant and smacked a bit of an inbred immodesty." His tone was light and there was a hint of humor behind it. But there was nothing casual about the way I felt.

"You were brave enough tonight," I answered, suddenly confused. I remembered back when we were on the plane together and everything he'd said was deliberately meant to irritate me. Now everything had changed. It was hard to think, hard to make conversation.

The silence grew thick and heavy between us. Unwilling to let him know I'd seen him earlier, I stammered a quick lie, "I—thought you were in Washington—"

"And until I saw you in the garden I thought you were in New York." Our eyes touched, separated quickly, and I laughed nervously. He walked with me to the stairs that curved up from the hall to my wing, and as I stood on the first step we were almost eye to eye. I held out my hand and said, "Well, thanks again for saving me from a fate worse than death. The next time I go walking I'll pick my district more carefully!" I felt a strange reluctance to leave. He took my hand and bent over it. "Good night, Dr. Blakley. It was a pleasure, I assure you. It's not often I've a chance to be a hero."

He turned and walked across the hall to the opposite stair. I leaned against the newel post and watched him. His stride was long and sure. He looked so—so British. Rather like a chameleon that changes colors to meet different environments. At the stairs he looked back. Our eyes met and neither of us turned away. There was nothing in the touch of our eyes to suggest a whisper of love. God, no! It was like a crash of thunder on a starlit night. A jagged bolt of lightning across a sky as black as death. A magnetism beyond anything I'd ever imagined pulled me through opening doors, and I cared not a whit whether they opened to Heaven or Hell.

I took a step toward him, then stopped. I felt my hand reach out to him. Then I took another step and another, until I'd crossed the hall and stood below him at the foot of the stairs. I hesitated then, looking up at him; my arms hung limp at my sides. His eyes were darker in the half-light of the room, and shadows from the hanging brass lamp crisscrossed his face. Neither of us smiled. Neither of us spoke. I couldn't. My breath was knotted in my throat.

He stood head and shoulders above me, and when he stooped to put his arm around me I stayed as I was. Only when he started up the stairs I moved as one with him. Lightly. Effortlessly. With no sense of steps or weight or time. He pushed open a door and we entered together. A half-conscious blur of a sitting room with soft carpets and low furniture and dim lights with a bedroom beyond crossed my vision before he closed the door behind us and touched his hand to my face.

His lips were hard and demanding, and I was transformed into a resilient mass that reacted to every touch—every movement of his hands, his lips, his body. There was no past, no present, no future. There was no Elizabeth Dameron with the same name as his. No Corraway Sheridan. No Sheridan Collection. No Bill Holmes. Only a vacuum that held me in its center. Only an unfamiliar demiworld in a birth of awakening new senses. The whole of me, my mind, my heart, my being, was in his possession. The feel and smell and taste of him was on my lips and my nostrils and my body. I knew that I was bewitched as surely as if a spell had been cast upon me, that I would never be whole again. As long as I lived, a part of me would always belong to this man. I'd stumbled into the scorpion's nest and was helpless.

Light years later, we lay silent—quiet. What words were spoken came slowly. I raised myself on one elbow and looked at him, at his eyes, soft now and full of love in the pale light. I touched his cheek with a finger and traced the crease that used to be a dimple. "The cards are stacked—you know everything about me. . . ." I whispered. He pulled my finger to his lips and kissed it. It was hard to keep talking when his lips were so close.

When I awoke, a flood of morning light touched the balcony and ran in horizontal lengths through half-pulled blinds across the wall and over the ceiling. I caught my breath remembering. Shards of splintered light cascaded over the bed and lay across his shoulders. The hairs on his arms shimmered gold. For a minute that seemed an eternity, I lay watching him. The easy breathing, the shadow of a beard along his cheeks, the crease that I felt the urge to touch again, his hair mussed and falling over his forehead. I wanted to cry.

He opened his eyes and looked at me. They were tawnier than ever, a deep gold-flecked brown, and the light that struck them from the window seemed to sink into their depths. They crinkled at the corners.

"Hello," he said.

I smiled at him and then lay back with my head on his shoulder. I belonged to this man and he to me. Whatever more could I ask of life. . . .

And from somewhere, my voice muffled in his neck, I asked, "Are you happy?"

And from somewhere far away he replied, "And what is happiness?"

I thought for a minute, wondering why he would answer my question with another, then answered, "Happiness is in giving—"

He interrupted. "There you have a Western woman's answer to what is happiness. It also answers other questions —and shows the difference between the Eastern woman and the Western woman."

Puzzled, I said, "I don't know what you mean."

"It's very simple . . . the Indian woman does not give herself for happiness—only in marriage. You say Western woman gives—for that is her happiness. I'd never thought of it that way."

I sat up quickly and said, "No—no, you don't understand—"

"But it's you who doesn't understand. Happiness can only come from oneself."

As he spoke, the first faint chill began to creep over me. "What *do* you mean?"

"It's clear enough, Bevan. It's the core of Hindu

philosophy—what Aubrey Menen calls 'The space within the heart.'" His eyes were level upon me. I made no reply, because I didn't know what to say. I felt only a terrible pulverizing fear. He turned on his back, put his arms under his head, and looked at the horizontal bars of sunlight that streaked the ceiling. Then he said thoughtfully, "Whenever the satisfaction of one's desires involve another, or whenever one's happiness depends on another, he becomes a prisoner. We cannot be ourselves when we are dependent on someone else. To a Hindu, happiness is not in giving ourselves, as you say—it's in being ourselves."

He turned to me then and smiled, his eyes crinkled, his face soft and loving. "Don't look so stricken, Bevan. I'm speaking as a Hindu man. Happiness is not a thing to be pursued. We are here—we accept. With you, your philosophy of living is different. You give. You are a nation of givers. You give your time to causes, you give your money to charities, and you—*you* give yourself."

I shook my head slowly when he paused. "No—oh, no—"

But he interrupted. "You say your happiness is giving. An Indian woman's, either Hindu or Moslem, is in a duty done—for her husband, her husband's parents, her children."

From far away I heard my voice small, unsteady. "And love has no place?"

"Duty, Bevan, is the word; the hub of the wheel. Duty to one's people, to one's children, to those who—who want to give."

My heart knotted up inside. My face felt frozen. I refused to believe what I heard him say. He couldn't seem to stop philosophizing, and everything he said twisted into me like a knife. "A Hindu feels pleasure or pain from outside stimuli—nothing more. For when a man has no wish for anything, neither happy with the good nor hating the bad, the wisdom of that man is proved. That, my dear, is from the *Gita*—"

"I know it's from the *Gita*," I answered quickly. "I'm the expert, the Western expert on Eastern philosophy—remember?" My voice was hard and brittle and I pulled the sheet up in front of me. "And so I'm that outside stimulus that has given you a night of pleasure. That's what you're saying—"

"A woman, Bevan, is God's gift to man and when she feels happiness in her gift, it is extremely pleasurable. . . ." He reached his arm around me and pulled me to him. I was as helpless as any fly in a spider's web. And I gave myself to him in a hopeless tangle of desire—despising it, despising the feeling I had for this man who possessed me, and who didn't given a damn.

Later with half-closed eyes I watched him shave and dress. Then he stooped over the bed to kiss me and didn't notice that I tightened every muscle in my face to keep from responding. He brushed his lips against my cheek and whispered in my ear, "It's altogether strange that you should give your gift first to me on the anniversary of my birth. Somehow I hadn't expected that I would be the first—I don't know why it should be so important to a Hindu. But it is. And I'll always wonder—" I kept my eyes closed. I heard the door open, and he said, "I'll be at Khilar most of the day. Ring for breakfast. I'll be back for tea. You'll be here, of course." I didn't answer. But when I heard the door close I crawled out of the bed feeling bruised and wounded. I dressed quickly in a frantic hurry to get out of the apartment.

I had to leave. Get away from Kataipur. Get away from Prakash Pita-Singh Vehta before he destroyed me. Because—because I loved him and he didn't love back. It was just as simple as that. Any woman—any woman at all would have pleased him last night. That was the galling bitter truth. Any woman at all.

I hurried down the stairs hoping I'd not see Bill or the desk clerk or any guests. There was a new man behind the desk and he watched me curiously as I crossed the hall and took the stairs to my wing, two at a time. I got out my key, opened the door, then closed it softly behind me and leaned against it. "You idiot—you solid gold, mink-lined, sterling idiot! Couldn't you have played a little harder to get? . . ." I crossed to the window and pulled up the blinds. I stood there looking over the garden but saw nothing. I held my eyes open wide; the breeze through the mulberry tree blew into them and dried the tears before they fell. I took a cold shower and scrubbed and scrubbed until my skin was raw, trying to scrape away the feel of him, the touch of him, the memory. . . .

Afterward I dropped the blinds and a cool darkness filled the room. I lay across the bed curled into a miserable knot and buried my head in the pillow, wishing I could cry. Wishing I could unravel my heart and wash the cinder-dry taste from my lips. But no tears came. I felt as if I was drying up. At some time I must have slept because I dreamed.

I dreamed that I came to the Khilar garden seeking Park. And there, surrounded by flowers that didn't smell, birds that didn't sing, butterflies that had no color, I found him. I called his name and hurried to him, but his eyes were cold and he turned away. Impulsively I put my hand on his arm as I'd done in the temple courtyard but he shook it off and walked away. I ran after him, calling to him, begging him to wait, but if he heard he made no sign. Then I stumbled and fell. I lay there for a long time, then suddenly I wasn't in the garden at all but lost in a vast red desert, and a cobra was shading me from a burning sun with his flared hood.

When I awoke a narrow edge of sunlight had broken through the blind, hurting my eyes; my throat was parched and I was gasping for air.

I splashed cold water onto my face trying to soothe my feverish eyes. Then I went downstairs. It was far into the morning and no one else was around. I got a cup of coffee and carried it into the garden. I wondered for a minute about Bill, then tried with a deliberate intensity to lose myself in the nearness of the garden. I forced myself to notice its flowers. I made myself feel its freshness. But all over I felt shriveled and drained. In my mouth, in my eyes, in my heart.

A kingfisher sat on a limb of an acacia tree, then as I watched he flew out of sight. The garden had just been sprinkled and in the shadows each blade of grass was tipped with a jeweled drop of water. A spider's web, each strand outlined with moisture, was stretched between hibiscus stalks. I watched with a morbid fascination as an insect with lovely irridescent colors struggled to free itself while the spider sat to one side watching. I picked up a twig and reached into the web and lifted the insect onto an acacia leaf. The spider rushed to the spot—and was already repairing the damaged web. I wanted to crush him but I—I could not. The small insect and I, we were both victims. If only someone could lift me as easily from the web that held me tangled, captive.

A chipmunk stood on its hind legs and regarded me intently. When he saw I had nothing to give him he scurried away, but without fear. I remembered the legend of how the Lord Rama had stroked the small creature and left the marks of his divine fingers along his back. The more I tried to think upon other things, the more Park intruded on my mind. The feel of him, the touch of him, the warm maleness of him, gripped my heart and wrung it dry.

I passed a niche in the garden wall where there was an image of the goddess Lakshmi, symbol of good fortune and love, who rose from the Churning of the Ocean bearing a lotus. Vishnu, upon seeing her, chose her for his own. Early Hindu kings were married to her at the same time they were married to their wives as a symbol of prosperity and good fortune, and the hope of siring many sons. This goddess of fertility was seated on a lotus leaf with miniature elephants on either side of her. She knows her own, I thought, and I'm not one of them. A bright bouquet of marigolds had been placed at her feet, someone's plea for love and prosperity. I stooped and picked a red marigold and placed it beside the others—but with little faith. . . .

I heard the crunch of gravel and looked up to see Bill walking toward me. "Where in the hell have you been?" he called. "I tried early this morning to get you and you were gone."

I avoided his eyes and shrugged. "I couldn't sleep. The garden's lovely, isn't it?" Then remembering what he said I asked, "Why did you want me?"

"I'm leaving tonight. My caravan with the statue got held up in the hills, and I've got to cross some palms with silver. I thought you might like to go with me."

"Oh, I'd like to—except I—" Suddenly I knew the only place I'd be safe from Park would be away from the Moti Palace. Of course I'd go—to the mountains, anywhere. "Well, really, there's nothing I can do about Elizabeth. When are you going?"

"I've hired a gharry. We'll leave the hotel after dark. We should be back about daylight."

"It sounds dangerous. Do you know where you're going?"

"Of course. And the boy driving has helped me many times before. It's Menon. He works part time at the hotel as clerk. You know him."

"Oh, yes. He told me he was a great friend of yours."

"That's right. He's helped get a lot of stuff out of India. And it's safe enough. It's not too far from here. I'd like to get the sculpture headed toward the railroad at Darampur. From there it can go by train to Calcutta. It'll stay in a warehouse there until I can get it on a boat to San Francisco. These mountain folk are interesting. You'll enjoy the whole thing."

"Bill, you're a lifesaver. I'll love going with you."

"We'll have dinner as usual, and then put on your darkest, warmest clothes. We'll meet Menon on the Kataipur road. Have you had breakfast?"

I shook my head. "I'm not hungry. I think I'll stay here awhile. But I'll see you tonight."

He turned to go, then I called him. "Bill, wait a minute. Do you know Prakash Pita-Singh—last name Vehta?"

"Damn right!"

"Who is he?"

"Well, he's the Maharaja's younger brother. And if the Maharaja's line dies out—as it looks like it's done— then he's the next one. Not that it means much any more. But they do control quite a fortune in Swiss banks, I hear. He's also the unofficial watchdog of Indian antiquities. He'll do damn near anything short of murder to keep Indian treasures here."

"Did you know he's just been at Midwestern University?"

He looked at me with quick interest. "No! Sheridan didn't say anything about it. Then he must have laid on the injunction!"

"That's what I think too."

"He's probably behind this snag of mine. If he is, money won't do a damn thing. But I have to try."

"While you're trying, see what Menon knows about Elizabeth. Miss Dameron has quite a pocketful, you know."

He nodded, his blue eyes bright as marbles in the morning sun. "I'll bet he can come up with something. We'll talk about it tonight. 'Bye now."

I listened to the crunch of his heels on the graveled path with a wry smile. I'd really hit botton, I thought, to be grateful for Bill Holmes.

I sat down on a bench backed against an acacia tree and tortured myself with memories I couldn't ignore. I'd heard, but never believed before, that India brings out concealed elements of one's personality. Then why in the hell did it wait six years to work on me! How could I —how could I—*how could I!* Like a woman of the Jamshed Road, where he found me, I'd gone to him. And though my heart was in my hand, he never noticed. And if he had, he'd have laughed. It would have made no difference. He thought like a Hindu. He was a Hindu. And I should have known.

Suddenly my mind stopped. I remembered for the first time since I left Uncle Coe—I remembered the Deccan *Katar* and I remembered the bet I'd made with Corraway Sheridan.

chapter VI

The memory of it twisted into me like the serrated edge of a knife. I doubled over with a very real pain and felt the blood drain from my face. I began to tremble and couldn't stop. *That was that he wanted.* He'd made it pointedly clear at the university and again on the plane to Washington that he'd stop at nothing to get the *Katar* and any other Indian treasures. And there was the injunction—certainly he was responsible for that. So it was neither me nor any other woman. He'd thought if I gave myself to him fully and without reservation, the *Katar* would fall quite naturally into his hands. And as a beautiful bonus probably the Emerald Kali, too. Because there was no doubt in my mind that he knew where she was. He knew everything about the Sheridan Collection.

I rose from the bench, my mind whirling bitterly. If he hadn't been so stupid—so—so Hindu—he would have gotten them too. If he had only said *I love you.* . . .

I bit my lip defiantly. At least he'd never get them

now. And if I couldn't have them because I'd fallen as stupidly as Uncle Coe had wanted me to, then they would be safe with him.

I walked aimlessly down a path to the native compound. Beside a gate was a small shrine built into the mud wall—the black goddess Kali. I stood looking at her for a minute. Goddess of destruction and rebirth. Here also there was a fresh offering of marigolds. Someone was covering his bets. I could do no less. I broke off a stem of red hibiscus and pulled the blossoms off one by one, placing them carefully around the feet of the goddess, burying Man, who lay beneath her foot, and the snakes that encircled him, under a mound of the blossoms.

For the life of me I couldn't have explained my actions. I felt destroyed, God knows. Not by this goddess, by a man. And I knew I'd never—there was no way—I'd never again look upon life the same as before.

I opened the gate and entered the compound. It was a world apart. The only thing of beauty were the vines that crept over the wall. There were bare earthen huts leaning against each other on the sunbaked ground, a few scrubby trees which had been born and lived voluntarily and looked ready to expire any day.

The difference between the garden with its fountains and flowers, its trees and deep shadows, and the scorched mud-walled enclosure was the difference between day and night. Wealth and poverty. Two sides of a darkly bright coin.

A bicycle tonga had been left at the garden gate. Probably a hotel employee. Only a few persons were about. A dhoti-clad man in a spotless muslin shirt was brushing his teeth over a dribbling faucet that made an irregular trickling stream through the dust and looked like blood. My, I thought, but you are morbid this morning. With good reason, I answered myself.

A couple of coarse-ribbed pi-dogs were snarling over a bone. A few scroungy chickens scratched in a dung pile where two small girls sat patting the dung into cakes for fuel. An old bull, the same color as the earth, rubbed against a scarred acacia tree. Then I saw the sadhu.

He was sitting cross-legged on a small platform inside a reed-covered shelter called an ashram. It was closed on three sides, open to the front where he meditated with his villagers. He was looking directly at me, straight across the compound yard, neither his eyes nor his expression wavering. It was as though he willed me to come, and, obedient as any worshipper, I went.

My smile was a sad one, I suspect, but I made the effort. "Good morning, *Panditji*, it is a far way from the Khilar Palace you are this morning." I spoke in Hindi. He answered in English.

"Yes, daughter, but not so far by boat. I knew you would be here, so it was that I made all necessary haste."

I looked at him, shaking my head. "*Panditji*, not even I knew that I would be here."

His expression didn't change. "You didn't know," he said, "but I did. I knew you would be in deep pain this morning and would come to me. Sit beside me, daughter, there are things I need to tell you."

I looked at him in wonder. How could this strange old man with the wrinkled face and long gray hair know that I had been crushed by this—this Eastern philosophy of theirs? And at the same time I felt a lifting of my spirit that was itself unexplainable. I placed my palms together and made an obeisance, then sat beside him on the rough woven mat. "*Panditji*, you are right. I need help."

"There is one who needs help more than you, daughter. The American princess you seek is beyond the Kalpa Lake—the smaller one called Manvantara. There, across the water, like stepping stones to heaven, are the Islands of Yuga. The largest is the ancient Shiva Temple. There you will find the princess with her ayah, Leela, and my brother. When you are with her, you will be healed of your own pain. She has great need of you."

I was listening to him with an intensity that strained every nerve, and when he paused I was silent for a minute. Then I asked, "What should I do, *Panditji?*"

"Pilgrims go one day a week. They leave from the water gate called Pearl. None except my brother and the Maharaja know that the princess is there."

"*Panditji*, is she all right?"

"She is in great danger, daughter. This is the day of the pilgrimage. The boat leaves from Moti Ghat. The pilgrims—the women—wear saffron saris and carry twists of the golden flower. Daughter, go now with our Lord Rama's blessing." He shifted his eyes away from me like a curtain falling and they stared in an unseeing trance toward the hills.

I rose quickly; chill bumps pricked my shoulders and I rubbed them nervously. Then standing before the sadhu I placed my palms together and bowed, whispering, "*Namaste, Panditji—*" He made no sign that he heard. I turned away from him and walked slowly to the gate.

Just inside stood a small girl with twin pigtails braided down her back, her eyes large and luminous. She was holding a package folded in woven banana leaves, and she shoved it into my hands and then ran back to the compound before I could speak.

Walking up the garden path with the strange package, remembering the holy man's counsel, I stopped. Then

I picked one more red hibiscus blosson freshly opened to the sun and carried it back to the Kali shrine. "I think we need you—Elizabeth and I." The thought was so strong I wasn't sure if I'd whispered it aloud or not. I laid the flower on top of the others. Then deciding that it's not only Hindus who cover their bets, I broke off a branch of jasmine and laid it in the niche of the Lakshmi Shrine beside the red marigolds.

Several guests were on the veranda when I returned, and I was relieved when I saw that Bill was not among them.

In my room I opened the package to find a saffron silk sari with a border of silver threads. With it, in a plastic bag speckled with spots of moisture, was a mala of pungent bright marigolds fully a meter long. I spent no time speculating where they'd come from. I knew. My meeting with the sadhu was one of those extraordinary events that have happened before to westerners in the East. And as others before me have learned, there are many things that are past understanding. That my wounded spirit was eased, I knew. But whether it was the temporary influence of the old sadhu, only time would tell.

Carrying the package tucked under my arm, I walked down the stairs with as casual an air as I could manage, hoping that I'd not see Bill. When I passed the bar, however, I heard his voice. I wouldn't have stopped—I'd have hurried by—except that I heard another one and recognized it.

It was impossible that they should be together. I walked to the door and glanced in. Bill and the Indian majordomo of Khilar Palace, the Maharaja's secretary, were seated at a small table by a garden window. I could tell Bill was angry, and surprised because it was the first time I'd seen him so. Their voices rose and they made no effort to lower them until Bill looked up and saw me. He stopped in the middle of a sentence, then started to his feet. But I waved and turned away. What had they been arguing about? I hadn't heard enough to have even a clue. But that they would know each other well enough to argue was the surprising thing. And why hadn't Bill said he knew him when I was describing my experience at the palace? Well, I'd find out tonight.

I passed the doorman and nodded, then walked down the palace road. I hoped I'd catch a ride after I reached the well-traveled Kataipur road, but if I didn't, it wouldn't be too long a walk. I'd taken it only last night—all the way to Jamshed Road. I had hardly turned onto the village road when a bicycle tonga pulled out from behind a multi-trunked banyan tree and stopped in front of me. "Meesy, Meesy," he called in a singsong inflection. "Jamel take Meesy, go Pearl Ghat—" He was a skinny little man wearing old army issue shorts that showed bulging leg muscles, and a ragged shirt with the sleeves torn out. His eyes were watery, his lips stained with betel juice. A gift from heaven, I decided promptly, and nodded. Then telling him to wait a second in Hindi, I stepped into the shadow of the banyan tree and draped the sari around me. I carried the plastic sack with the marigold wreath and left the small woven box behind.

The tonga-wallah showed no surprise when I reappeared. I climbed into the carriage, wondering if by chance this might be a gift, not from heaven, but from the old sadhu?

We were nearing Kataipur with a slow-moving traffic of bullock carts, donkeys, camels, and men, easing our way through them, when the arrogant honking of an automobile made us all scatter. A limousine met us, barely slackening its speed, showering us all with a thick layer of dust. I didn't have to see its red license plate to know it was from Khilar Palace, the same Rolls that had brought me back to the hotel. I felt a stifling resentment against the Sikh chauffeur and his passenger: I could no more help the aching stab in my chest than I could help breathing the red dust he left behind him.

The Pearl Ghat was a series of broad marble steps where the crystal-clean waters of the Pearl cascaded into the Kalpa. Hundreds of women, their saris gathered to their knees, were there beating their clothes with wooden paddles.

It was the constant slap-beat-slap that I had been conscious of when I awakened yesterday. Now the monotonous rhythm drummed into my head until I thought it would burst.

The motor launch, if it could be dignified by such a title, was alongside a sagging pier. There was no need to tell the tonga-wallah to stop. He knew exactly where he was to take me. I paid him rupees forty which he accepted with a snaggletoothed grin. "Memsab, when sun touches top of western hill I return for you." I thanked him and added, in Hindi, "May your road be smooth, Brother."

In the midmorning sun the lake flicked and shimmered from the current of the Pearl River, but beyond, it smoothed into marbled streaks of turquoise and applegreen jade that dimmed at the far bank where it paled into the paler hills.

Scattered fishing boats, flat brown-sailed skiffs, looked as though they had been painted onto a mirrored sea. Straggling groups of pilgrims walked toward the dock. Some stopped in small knots of orange and white beneath the neem trees across the road. Others bought soft drinks in paper cups. Each woman wore a saffron sari and the men were in spotless white dhotis, muslin shirts, and yellow turbans. The women outnumbered the men four to one. Both men and women carried *malas* of marigolds that gave a heady musky fragrance to the dock.

The instant I stepped from the tonga I lost my identity. I blended with the other pilgrims as smoothly as if I'd been wearing a sari all my life, making pilgrimages to shrines each week. My hair was parted in the middle and pulled back with a rubber band. By draping the end of the sari over my head, I could pass muster in any Hindu gathering. However, I stayed to myself, doing my best to look preoccupied in holy meditation. When there were fifty or so waiting, a sailor who had been sitting on the dock climbed on board the launch and pulled a small steam whistle. Another sailor in soiled white jodhpur pants and turban revved the motor, which coughed a time or two, then belched a series of black smoke rings from its stack amidship.

I stood well back in line, observing the proper procedure, and at the same time having second thoughts about getting on this infirm vessel. The excursion was cheap enough, rupees ten for a round trip. I followed an old woman onto the launch. Hard benches lined the fore and after decks under a stained canvas awning. The craft vibrated noisily, and when the last of the pilgrims were seated, the railing was snapped over the gangway, the line cast off, and we sputtered away from the dock. The motor turned heavily, churning an irregular wake behind us. We curved slowly in a wide port arc toward the far bank of the lake, leaving a trail of doughnut-shaped clouds that drifted back toward Kataipur.

We hugged the shoreline, and I wondered if the captain and his crew didn't have the same distrust of their boat that I had. Eventually we were in the shadow of the palace wall, but search as I might, I couldn't find the lake entrance to the garden I'd seen the day before. Shortly after we reached the end of the red stone ramparts, we had a splendid view of the ruins of the old fort. Its towers stood disheveled and uneven and its great wall grew up from the lake as though it had been nurtured by it. The Maharaja's personal standard flew from the highest tower.

It wasn't long until we came to the locks and it took only minutes to be lowered into Lake Manvantara. The islands, "the Stepping Stones," stretched across the lake in symmetrical order like so many giant brown turtles. As we chugged past I saw an occasional shack or fishing skiff, sometimes a small whitewashed shrine. The launch with its boiling wake stirred enough breeze to make me feel chilled.

I sat on the hard wooden bench pressed closely against my neighbors. The last island began taking shape. As we neared, I could see it was covered with a temple that seemed to spread up, over, and around its marble buttresses that swept into the lake. And from strange little corners in every direction up and down there sprouted a tree or bush.

The boat moored at a narrow wooden dock, which was set on uneven pilings that dipped and swayed as the pilgrims disembarked. It led to steep marble steps that climbed out of the clear green water toward the temple, and I knew that they had been carved out of the heart of the island even before Akbar had made his imprint on Northern India.

Climbing the flight of stairs the pilgrims wound above me like a long yellow serpent. I stayed behind to let the others go ahead, then I followed.

At the top of the steps, a hundred or more feet above

the landing where a broad flagged terrace circled the temple, sat a frail ascetic-looking sadhu. He was on a low platform, beneath a reed umbrella, in the Padmasana pose; legs tucked under him, feet on his thighs, his hands palm upwards on his knees. His eyes wide open stared unblinking straight through me. He, too, was almost naked, his body smeared with ashes, his hair gray and matted, hanging below his shoulders, a near replica of my friend the old sadhu. There was a wooden begging bowl and a small heap of wild flowers beside him.

I pinched a marigold from the *mala* and added it to the little mound of flowers. He never looked at me. He never moved, not even the flicker of an eyelid. His spirit, his mind, his soul were as far from his emaciated body as the farthest cloud-tipped mountain peak. And a bit of the wonder and awe that man has ever held for holy things touched me and I wished I had more to give than a pinched-off wilted flower. I placed my palms together and whispered, *"Namaste, Pitaji."*

A saffron-clad woman separated herself from the serpentine line twisting into the temple and came to meet me. She was very old. Her hair was white and stood stiffly away from her face and fastened into a thin knot on her neck. Her brown face was crisscrossed with thousands of sun-dried wrinkles. She motioned to me and we brought up the end of the pilgrims' procession.

I followed the old woman into the courtyard where the other pilgrims had shed their shoes. She turned, leading me through a narrow archway, and opened a heavy wooden door. I followed her with a blind trust through semidark corridors that were cool and smelled of age-old dust and emptiness. There was priceless art on every hand. Lord Shiva in every possible pose and reincarnation with Parvati in her other manifestations, as Kali and Durga.

Sandstone carvings, wooden sculptures, and reliefs of Lord Rama and Lord Krishna filled every possible space on the walls. This was one temple whose artifacts hadn't been plundered. We climbed countless series of stairs, and occasionally I'd see a glimpse of the lake through narrow arched windows and get a breath of fresh lake air. Finally she held out her hand to guide me, then pushed open a wooden door with heavy brass fittings.

This is Elizabeth's prison, I thought, and suddenly I was frightened. I'd concentrated so hard on getting here that I hadn't thought what I would say when I saw her. Would she have changed? Well, of course.

The room we entered was as lovely as any I'd ever seen. A silky seventeenth-century Anatolian rug with its blues and yellows and reds, as fresh and clear as when it was woven, covered the greater part of the marble floor. Low chairs with soft cushions in shades of pink and red made it a warm room. A heavily encrusted ormolu table held a Tiffany oil lamp and through double doors I saw a balcony partially screened with exquisite marble fretwork. It looked like something out of the *Arabian Nights,* and I began to envy her her prison. The old lady motioned for me to sit, but I was too restless. I walked to the balcony, then turned so that I could see the door where Elizabeth would enter. I remembered the sari and took it off, dropping it and the rope of marigolds over the back of a chair. I pulled the rubber band from my hair to let it fall loose. At least I wanted Elizabeth to see someone who looked like—well, like home.

I was nervous. My palms were damp. I had never been gracious to Elizabeth and now the memory came back to haunt me. Suppose she refused to see me? Suppose she—

I heard the door and turned around. She stood in the

archway, a white silhouette against the darkness behind her, and I choked. She was in the last stages of pregnancy.

"Elizabeth, it's me—Bevan Blakley, from Midwestern University." I decided suddenly that she might not recognize me, or that she might have forgotten—

"I know, Dr. Blakley. I knew you were here."

I started to go to her; I wanted to embrace her. Instead I said, "Elizabeth, we've been worried. How are you?"

She let me take her hand when I reached for it, but it was limp. I gave it a quick squeeze and let it drop. She wore a white sari, a sign of widowhood. Her hair was parted in the center and hung in one thick golden-brown braid down her back. The fact that it was a dark blond for some reason didn't make her look less Indian. There was an orange tilak between her eyebrows. She looked at me with level green eyes shadowed with lashes so thick and dark they looked as if they were rimmed with khol. There was no expression at all in them. Had she been drugged?

"Elizabeth, will you send the ayah away so we can talk?"

She turned slowly and spoke to the old woman in Hindi, who ducked her head obediently and left the room. Then I followed Elizabeth to the balcony. We stood at the waist-high balustrade and looked down on the lake. From such a height it was indigo. A jagged white scar followed the pilgrim launch, chugging back toward Kataipur for more pilgrims. Haloed smoke rings drifted over the water. A brisk breeze, cool and sweet from the hills, tangled my hair and billowed her sari. She smiled with her lips, not her eyes.

"It—it's good of you to come. How is Auntie?" Her English sounded stilted as though she hadn't been accustomed to using it.

"Terribly worried about you. Why haven't you written?"

"I can't—I couldn't—"

"Are you a prisoner?"

She shrugged, then sighed. "I don't know." Then she repeated it softly. "I truly don't know."

"You must have a better explanation than that."

"The baby." She rubbed her hand across the bulging sari. "The baby must be protected—"

"Against whom?" I had to struggle to get the slightest response.

She shook her head.

"Elizabeth," I tried to catch her eye and couldn't. "I must know—Jai, where is he?"

"Dead." Her voice was flat and unemotional.

"But how?"

"I don't know. I just don't know."

I felt as if I were trying to hold a trailing vapor of smoke in both hands. That I was an inquisitor prying into something I had no business to know. But I had to keep on. "Do you know that they say you—you did it?"

"Yes." Her answer was a breath of air expelled quickly. She didn't look at me, only at the lake below and there was nothing there except its dark blue surface with the faint curving line of turquoise that trailed the launch.

"Elizabeth, I have to know, so that I can help you. Did you—did you—?"

"I don't know."

"You have to know!" My voice sounded harsh to my ears. Harsh and despairing. But hers never changed inflection.

"I don't know. . . ." she repeated in her deadly monotone.

I turned away from the window to stare at her. "Have you been drugged?"

"I don't know."

"How long ago did Jai die?"

"I don't know."

I felt frustrated and dug my fingernails into the palms of my hands. I wanted to scream at her, *Wake up! Do SOMETHING! Stop this passive acceptance of whatever is tearing at you.*

"Elizabeth," I said slowly, trying to reach her, desperately trying to keep the rising panic I felt out of my voice, "I'm here to help you. When is the baby due?"

"I don't know."

I grabbed her arm. "Elizabeth, you have to know. Is it soon?"

She pulled away from me and walked to a secluded corner of the balcony, then reached beneath her sari and drew out a small bag. "Will you—will you do this for me?" She pulled a crushed yellow-red marigold from the sack and handed it to me. "Take my flower and go to the Kali Temple on any day except Tuesday or Saturday. Buy a sacrificial plate—you'll see a young boy selling them for one or two rupees. Add this flower to it. Give the priest rupees ten and the holy man rupees five and . . . ." She hesitated, then pressed the flower in my hand just as the ayah came onto the balcony. I slipped the flower into the pocket of my dress.

The ayah spoke to Elizabeth who turned to me. "Leela has tea and sweetmeats. I'll have her bring them here."

The old woman set the tray on a low brass table and pulled up chairs for us, then left. Elizabeth poured a cup of tea, then put down the pot and looked at me.

"Perhaps it is drugged," she said. "I hadn't thought

of it before. I've trusted Leela completely. She was Jai's nurse when he was a baby." She pushed her chair back, walked to the balustrade, and leaned against it, looking over the lake to the pale blue hills with blank unseeing eyes. "You know, they say I killed Jai. I don't know. I loved him so much it's hard for me to believe that I did— but I don't remember."

"Who are *they?* Who say you did?"

"Everybody . . ."

"That's a little vague."

"Well, of course the officers—I don't know who they were. Someone from Darampur and from Kataipur. Then the old Raja and his secretary." She touched her hand to her forehead as though trying to clear cloudy memories. "I don't know. It doesn't make sense, any of it. Jai was his father's heir. The Raja is so old he isn't going to live long. With Jai alive I had everything to look forward to—without him, nothing. I have nothing. I am nothing." Her gaze shifted to the floor where the sun shone obliquely through the marble fretwork making stylized shadow patterns on the floor. I didn't answer because I didn't know what to say.

In a low monotone, still staring at the floor, she continued. "So many tragedies. Durga dying near Bangladesh. Bhimi in an airplane crash. Jai. Now three widows." She stopped then to look at me and her eyes seemed to clear, almost as if a fog lifted from them. "Dr. Blakley, Kataipur is different from the rest of India. There is nothing about the New India here. It's lost in the foothills of the mountains. Everything is contradictory. The old Raja sent his sons to England to be educated, but not his daughters. They were betrothed as infants and married as children. The sons he prepared for a modern world, but married them to children as uneducated as his daughters. He believes in purdah for women; there is even a zenana at Khilar."

"A zenana? You mean that today—there is still a section of the palace for the women only? That's hard to believe—"

"It's true. Where the women are kept. And that's the word I mean—*kept*. Where the old Raja has his wives, and where the widows live, and the young girls until they marry. Can you believe the widows—the three of us—will never be seen by a man again? Never remarry or have children?"

"No, I really can't. It's—medieval."

She gave a brief bitter laugh. "We should be grateful, I suppose. Jai's great-grandmother committed suttee when the Jat Pita-Singh died."

"Oh, that's been outlawed for a hundred and fifty years—"

"Well, this was a hundred years ago and she's the heroine of Khilar. There are paintings of her all over. To inspire the occupants of the zenana, I suppose."

"Were you there, in the—that place?" I felt a smothering horror that Elizabeth had been closed up in a palace harem.

"Yes, until they brought me here."

I clasped my hands together and pulled hard until I though I'd break my fingers. "God!" I took a deep long breath and expelled it slowly, then said in as normal a voice as I could find, "I was at the palace yesterday—"

"At Khilar," she interrupted. Her eyes were full of shadows. "Yes, I knew. I was surprised they let you in."

"They barely did. He wouldn't tell me where you were except that you were in custody. A strange man with peculiar eyes."

"That's Deleep Chatterjee. He's secretary to the Raja

and runs the palace. I've always been a little afraid of him. No, not afraid exactly. He's a servant, but he—he intimidated me."

"He did me too." I looked at her and tried to smile. But I knew it was a sick attempt. I took the teapot and the cup of cold tea and emptied them into an earthenware urn that had bougainvillea climbing out of it. "That takes care of that. I hope it doesn't kill the plant." I replaced the pot and cup on the tray, then asked, "How did you know I was in Kataipur?"

"I knew as soon as you arrived in Delhi. The sadhu was waiting for you at Khilar."

I looked at her astonished. "Why, that's not possible."

"You'll learn that many things are possible here. There is no way for the old sadhu to communicate with the holy man here—but he does. Don't ask me how. It's past all understanding. They seem to communicate through ESP. But I'm grateful for the holy man here at the temple. He's—well, he's just here, and I'm glad."

I told her how I'd learned where she was through the old sadhu. Then I said, "But you know, this doesn't seem like a prison—"

"Of course it's not really. I'm here so the baby will be protected. The Raja doesn't want anything to happen to me until after the baby comes."

I caught the implication of her meaning, but before I could question her she suddenly began talking—not really to me, more to herself. I listened and didn't interrupt. "Jai left Midwestern University to come back and marry the child he'd been betrothed to when she was born. He was only thirteen then. He was twenty-six when he returned and of course had never seen her.

"They had a royal wedding which took place with the stars in their most favorable context and you can imagine how distasteful it all was to Jai, brought up in a Western world—a brilliant student, a Ph.D., an outgoing man with a total Western culture—" She stopped abruptly and shook her head. "No, it wasn't total. It was a veneer, but it hadn't been scratched then. The wedding lasted for days, then he brought her here and she was frightened to death. So the wedding wasn't consummated when it should have been. Jai installed her in an apartment where she played with Durga's son, Krishna, and his sister, and Bhimi's little daughters while Jai waited for her to grow up.

"She was a Rajasthan princess and the old Raja discussed it with her father who was a prince in a northwestern province. Of course, if they'd sent her home it would have been a terrible disgrace. So things rocked along for a year, and then I won the Sheridan scholarship and came to Delhi." She looked at me with a half-smile. "You know, Dr. Blakley," she interrupted herself, "there was no way that I could come to India and not let Jai know."

As she spoke I was remembering. Remembering their love affair on the campus of the university. Remembering the times Elizabeth would come to my studio to talk about India, when it was Jai that she really wanted to talk about. And I remembered my antagonism toward her and knew that Elizabeth remembered too. I felt it in her dignity, in the labored use of my title.

I looked at her gravely. "Elizabeth, I wish you would call me Bevan."

She smiled then and it was like seeing a flower blossom. "I'd like to—Bevan."

I reached out and touched her arm softly, then said, "So you wrote him you were coming."

"Yes. He was at the airport to meet me." A little

color came into her cheeks and she seemed to glow at the memory. "He was working with the government in the agricultural department, a strange place for a philosophy major, but he wanted to help his people in Kataipur and was learning as he worked. So we had an apartment there and I loved it.

"Then his father called him home to do something about his marriage, and this time I don't know if Jai deliberately tried to drive the girl away from him or not. He didn't love her, wanted nothing to do with her, and when she became hysterical again, he told his father it was impossible. So they made arrangements to send her back, return the dowry and everything. The girl's father was furious. Then the girl took sick, and before the dowry could be returned she died."

A startled gasp slipped from me, but Elizabeth went on quickly as though she was anxious to get the story over. "Her family blamed the old Raja and swore she had been poisoned. They also demanded that the dowry be returned. Well, no one knew if she had been or not. She was cremated at the family ghat and there was no thought of an autopsy. The Raja refused to return the dowry.

"So then Jai came back to Delhi. All this time I was really working—studying Indian history, Rabindra literature, everything of Tagore's—Hindi and Bengali. I never mentioned marriage to Jai. I was happy the way things were, but he decided we should be married. So he approached his father. . . ." She smiled grimly and shook her head when she caught my eye. "You can imagine what happened. The Raja threatened to disinherit him and called me every dreadful name you've ever heard of. It seems he knew all about our life together in Delhi—but considered me a part of Jai's extracurricular activities. Then about that time Durga was killed in a skirmish at

Bangladesh. He was a lieutenant colonel in the army. That was a terrible blow to the Raja and Bhimi, and to Jai. The brothers were good friends. Then Bhimi was flying to England on a state mission and the plane crashed. That left only Jai and the young boy, Krishna, who was heir to the throne." A shadow crossed her face and I knew it was painful for her to think about the child. But she didn't mention his death. She was telling her story in sequence, and I listened as she continued.

"Then one day he came to me and said, 'I'm sick of this. I don't give a damn what the Raja says, we're going to be married.' So we were. In a legal ceremony which, of course, had no relation to astrology or whether it was the proper time or not. And if you know India—and you do—nothing is done, certainly nothing so important as a wedding, without giving due thought to what the stars have in mind for your future. We simply got married and then Jai told his father. The old Raja never did accept me. Still I tried to become Hindu in every way. Religion," she lifted the silver lingam that hung around her neck, "language, customs, dress." She stopped suddenly, glanced at me quickly and then back toward the hills. She looked pale and defeated and her voice was only a whisper. "There is no way, Bevan, a person can become a Hindu if he's not born one. You can become a Catholic or a Methodist or a Moslem, or even a Jew, but don't ever let anyone tell you that you can be converted to Hinduism. It's impossible. There is no creed, no ritual, there are a thousand meanings, each saying something different to the person listening. I tried and failed."

For a long time neither of us spoke, then she took up her story again. "And so I came into the palace. Suddenly all the astrologers in Kataipur began telling the Raja that I was a dreadful catastrophe, that the wedding would bring fire, flood, famine, and death. Jai and I laughed about it, and even the old Raja, to give him credit, shrugged it off. But the widows didn't. I saw them often. There wasn't much to do and, trying to please the old Raja, I kept to the women's quarters except when Jai was home. We had our own apartment in the palace.

"I loved the children. There are four little girls, then there was the boy, Krishna, Durga's son who became the Maharaja's heir. He was ten, a charming boy, the only one in the palace who accepted me. He died a dreadful death from the cobra in the garden." Her voice broke and she covered her mouth with the pallav of her sari. It was the first time she had shown any emotion since I'd been there.

"I loved him, Bevan. I loved the little boy so much that Jai couldn't understand it. And now everyone is dead. The widows and their little daughters live in seclusion at Khilar. The girls will escape only when they are married and then into another zenana ruled by a vindictive old woman. The widows never will—"

"And you were all there together?"

She nodded. "It was terrible. Much better to have been in Delhi, unmarried. Jai was still working for the government there and I was left in the palace with all those women. I tried to organize classes in English and painting. The children were talented, but the Maharaja got word and made me stop." She drew a long tired breath and expelled it slowly. "There was one old woman there, Bevan, the Rani Asha, who understood. She had been well-educated, but tried to hide it. I guess there'd be no living with the others if she couldn't be like them. She hadn't been outside the zenana in thirty years. Can you imagine? Well, I was going crazy. I had to do something, so I began to study religion. I would come here every Saturday with the pilgrims, and on other days, except Tuesdays, I went to the Kali Temple in the mountains. That was where the old sadhu stayed. He had an ashram there and a few disciples and I would sit by the hour and listen to him read from the *Bhagavad-Gita* and the *Ramayana* and the *Upanishads*. He's the one who sent you to me."

"Yes. I gave him my coral necklace and asked for his blessing."

She looked at me and smiled. Then she reached into her sari and pulled out the necklace. "Is this it?"

I stared at her. "How did you get it?"

"The old sadhu sent it. I'm not going to give it back to you. It's been blessed and God knows I need something to hang onto besides this." She touched the lingam that swung on a silver chain, lost in the folds of the sari. "And then," she continued, "I found I was pregnant. Of course, Jai and I were happy. The others? Well—I don't know. I couldn't go to the mountain shrine any more, or to the village and take the launch here. I was terribly sick. So nauseated." She rested a second before she continued. "Jai was still working in Delhi, but after Bhimi was killed, he came back to Khilar. And, Bevan, the veneer—the Western veneer—had rubbed off. He brought a woman, a young girl, Madhuri, back with him." She swallowed hard and then continued, still looking across the lake with clouded eyes. "He installed her in a suite above our apartment and sent me to the zenana to stay."

I felt my lips draw tight. "How awful. How terrible for you!"

"You can't know. It was hell. Pure hell. He tried to tell me it wasn't because he loved me less, but that it was the thing to do while I was carrying the child. Nothing I could say would make him send her away. After the first three months I began to feel better and I insisted on going back to the temple—"

"Which temple?" I interrupted.

"The Kali Temple, in the mountains. It was the only way I could escape from the palace even for a few hours. I'd wear a burqa—to cover my face even in the temple— and I never saw Jai. He ignored my requests—oh God, Bevan, more than requests, I begged him to see me, I wrote him, I sent him messages. And I never saw him again until the last time I returned from the mountain shrine. I was in—" she put her hand to her head and rubbed her forehead. "I wish I could remember. I know I went to the apartment. It was the first time I'd been there in months—"

"Yours and Jai's?"

"Yes. I was—I don't know why I was there. I had the marigold mala the priest had given me and the cake, the ghee and honey rice cake, and the flower and the ribbons—" She seemed to be mentally counting on her fingers. "I put them on the gallery ledge and was raising the blinds when someone came in. I thought it was Jai. I remember turning around and was surprised to see Deleep. He said Jai wanted to see me upstairs. That, of course, would be in Madhuri's apartment. Everyone—all the widows and Jai's stepmothers and the nieces—had gone to great lengths to tell me how beautiful she was. Well, that's all I remember, telling Deleep I didn't want to go there—that I'd return to the zenana." She stopped talking and leaned her head against the marble fretwork. It felt cold to my hand even with the sun against it.

"Then what happened?" I asked. My mouth was dry.

"I don't know. There's a gap there I simply can't remember. I was talking to Deleep, and the next thing I was in Madhuri's bedroom looking down at Jai on Madhuri's bed. I had a dagger in my hand. He was bleeding and trying to say something, and blood ran from his mouth—Oh, God, Bevan, do you know that I held the Deccan *Katar* in my hand! I don't know where it came from, but it was identical to yours—the very same. I didn't really see it until the servants came in and took it from me and by then Jai was dead—and then I must have fainted. . . ."

I stared at her, unable to speak. I remembered back to Lane Thomas' office at Midwestern University when he said, "Mr. Pita-Singh wants to buy your Deccan *Katar*. *It's one of a pair that belonged to the Maharaja.*"

Finally I found my voice. "Have you . . . have you seen it since?"

She shook her head slowly.

"Where was Madhuri?"

"She wasn't there. The next day—maybe the next or the next, I can't remember—there was the funeral. I stood on the balcony in the zenana and watched the smoke curl up from the river. Then the Raja had me brought here."

"Was there a trial?"

"I don't think so. I—can you believe that I really don't know?"

"Yes, Elizabeth, I can. I'm going to take you to the hotel and we'll fly back home immediately."

"No, I can't do that. I will stay here until the baby is born, and then I have to die." She said it matter-of-factly as someone would say, "After the baby is born, I have to go to Chicago." It took a second or two before it penetrated my brain.

"Oh, no! Elizabeth, of course not!"

"Yes. The Raja wants the baby—that is, if it's a boy. They don't give a damn about it if it's a girl. She'll probably go with me. But it's a boy. I know. The sadhu said so—" Suddenly she smiled. "Look, feel—he's jumping. Ah! The little Raja wants out of there."

I couldn't look at her as I put my hand on her abdomen and felt the feathery movement of the fetus. "I hope I get to see him," she said slowly. "I don't want to die until I've held him."

I grabbed her shoulders with both hands and shook her. "Stop talking like that! Nothing's going to happen to you. I won't let it!"

"Bevan." She seemed strangely calm. "Don't worry about me. There is nothing that can be done." Then she smiled and added, "It's all written in the stars, you see. You may laugh at those things, but I've had a little experience with their truth since I've been at Khilar. Everything—everything is in the stars. It's an ancient science."

"All right, I agree; it's an ancient science and God knows, Elizabeth, I'm not laughing. Will you have the baby here?"

"No, the Raja will send for me when the time comes."

"And I suppose they know that from the stars too?"

She shrugged unsmiling. "I don't know. I've lost track of time. He's getting heavy."

"I don't understand why the Raja had you sent here."

"As I said, to protect the baby."

"Who would want to hurt him?"

She looked over the lake and her voice was tired. "There is someone, but that's another story. Family jealousy. The Maharaja's brother, Prakash, of course."

chapter VII

My fingers gripped the marble fretwork until I thought I would have to pry them loose. I felt the blood drain from my face. *Calm. I must be calm—she mustn't know.* And in an icy voice that seemed to come from another person I asked, "Why—why would he want—" I couldn't finish the question. It was impossible for me to form the words.

But Elizabeth didn't notice and answered as if I had. "The Raja knows Prakash wants the throne. He's wealthy in his own right. He was reared in England too, like his nephews, and he has just the same polished Western veneer that they all have. He's older; he has a cosmopolitan manner, and the only thing he doesn't have is the power and the prestige that is the inherited right of the Maharaja. There is only the little Raja here," she placed her hand on her bulging abdomen, "between him and the Ivory Throne of Maharaja Hari Pita-Singh."

"You have to be mistaken." Finally I found my voice;

it was thin and weak. I turned from the balustrade. "The Raja must have a vivid imagination—and he must hate his brother very much."

"No, Bevan." The pattern of the fretted shadows made the light break across her face like a jigsaw puzzle. "No, it's true. Everyone knows that he was in the garden just before Krishna was struck by the snake. You see, the cobra is a very old and a very gentle snake. He had to be provoked into striking the boy."

"I can't believe anyone—"

"Oh, but there's more. Prakash was booked to fly from Delhi to England. Then he talked Bhimi into going and he was to take a later plane. His luggage was still on board." She looked at me and her insinuation was clear enough.

"You make him sound like a monster, Elizabeth—" The feeling I had for him was as strange as the fear Elizabeth and I shared for the man—yet I felt a compulsive urgency to defend him. "That simply is no proof!" I said.

"It's enough for me. I hate him and I'm afraid of him. Bevan, stay with me until my baby is born. Help him—"

I began crying then. No sobs or wracking emotion, only tears that streamed from my eyes with no beginning and no ending. I leaned my head against the cool marble and watched them fall on the balustrade. All those tears I'd wanted to shed this morning, all the tears I'd dammed up, fell now, and I made no effort to control them. Elizabeth took me in her arms and comforted me because she thought I wept for her. For her and her unborn child.

Leela came in. "The pilgrims—the last boat, Missy. You go now and come next week?"

I nodded wearily and took the handkerchief she offered to dry my eyes. Leela picked up the sari and draped it around me. I handed the marigold mala to Elizabeth.

"Give this to Lord Shiva when the others have gone. I'll come—I'll come when I can."

She put her arms around me and kissed me on both cheeks. "Dear Dr. Blakley—Bevan—to come so far. Write Auntie and tell her I'm well and that I love her. She seems light years away."

"She is," I replied. Then I turned quickly to follow Leela through the maze of the temple. A lingering good-bye would have unraveled me completely.

The ayah opened the final door and motioned me through. She stayed behind and I walked back to kiss her cheek. "Be good to her, Little Mother," I said, "she needs a friend."

I dropped some coins into the begging bowl of the old sadhu as I passed and saw the flicker of an eyelid. "She needs a double blessing, *Pitaji*," I whispered, "she and the baby." Then I hurried down the steep steps and was the last to climb aboard.

As soon as we cleared the dock I looked up to the heights of the temple, and far to the left I thought I saw a shadow on the balcony. The journey back to the Pearl Ghat was a wretched trip filled with tangled thoughts.

How could I ever forgive myself for the wrong I had done Elizabeth so many years before? I searched my heart wondering *why?* Had I been possessed of some frightful jealousy, some fear that this beautiful girl with her talent and name would supplant me at the university? I leaned back against the hard-edged bench and closed my eyes and let the wind whip across my face. Whatever it had been, it was gone now, and only a full, overriding love for this brave girl was left in its place.

I rehashed everything Elizabeth had said, her fear for the baby, her fear of Prakash— She had to be wrong! She had to be—*she had to be—*

Jamel was waiting as he'd promised, and I climbed into the carriage. We worked our way through the town to the Moti Palace road. Then I remembered the flower Elizabeth had given me.

"Do you know the Kali shrine?" I asked.

"Ah, yes, Meesy, I know," he answered, nodding as his muscular legs moved the pedals of the bicycle as automatically as pistons. "You will go tomorrow?"

I thought quickly. Today was Saturday. Had I left the university only a week ago? A lifetime—two lifetimes ago? Two lifetimes that had changed my own as inexorably as if day had ceased to follow night and there was only a nightmare world to live in.

There was no part of this journey that paralleled in any way the years I'd spent in India. How young I had been! Then I'd skimmed across the top of a society, mouthing slick-sounding phrases—India, indestructible India. As full of time as time itself. Relentlessly feeding upon itself. One thousand years the same, yet constantly changing. Ten million lives renewing themselves in a philosophy so ancient that Plato was a believer. Fly specks on the turning wheel. I had acquired a superficial knowledge in shallow fields, believing I was studying the culture of a people. I couldn't have been more wrong. I had been in a land of violent contrasts, but those contrasts failed to touch me. Now the contrasts had not only touched me. They wanted to destroy me. Me and Elizabeth.

Six years ago I had stared curiously while fanatic worshippers at the Kali Temple in Calcutta touched sacrificial blood to their foreheads and lips, kneeling in front of a sacred phallus while a priest chanted prayers and touched it with clarified butter, and I had neither sympathy nor understanding. Now Elizabeth was one of them. Elizabeth from Midwestern University, as American as apple pie, wearing a lingam fertility symbol, an orange tilak of the Kali cult, and instructed by an ash-smeared sadhu.

And if I'd been too young six years ago to grasp the social significance of a people in flux, I wasn't now. In the old Maharaja I understood the crisis of a man facing a world whose structure he sees, but whose spirit escapes him. So he sent his sons into a civilization he refused to allow them to bring back. And his women he kept as separated as his father and his grandfather and his great-grandfather had before him. Now his kingdom hung about his head in tangled threads with only one small spindle—yet unborn—to hold it together.

The men in his family had been educated into pseudo-Englishmen, with a veneer of Western civilization that scratched as easily as cheap enamel. Elizabeth had discovered it; so had I: she in her way and I in mine. In our naïve Western fashion we'd thought love, and the desire that was a part of it, synonymous with happiness. But it was truly the opposite. Elizabeth was in a hell of her own and I was in mine. We had opened those doors to our private hells ourselves and entered them of our own accord—nothing could change that. Our hells were of our own making. We had built the walls and stoked the fires and opened the dampers wide to make our own pact with our separate devils and now we would be destroyed.

The tonga-wallah pedalled along placidly, occasionally looking back waiting for an answer. "Yes," I said, "tomorrow morning."

"Early?" he asked.

Having no idea how long it would take, I replied, "Yes, early. Can you get a gharry?"

He flashed his betel-lipped, jagged-toothed smile back at me and nodded vigorously. A bicycle tonga is no vehicle to take up in the mountains.

He pulled under the banyan tree and I slipped out of the yellow sari, folded it carefully and laid it on the seat beside me. A few minutes later we'd turned into the Moti Palace driveway. The hotel guests were having tea on the hotel veranda when I returned, Bill with them. He waved as we rode up and I dreaded to talk with him. I was as unnerved as if I'd been through an earthquake, and I very nearly had. I wished he wasn't here, or hadn't seen me. I couldn't talk about Elizabeth. Not yet. Then suddenly I remembered that I was supposed to go to the mountains with him. I couldn't go to the Kali shrine in the morning. I touched the wallah on the shoulder and said, "I've forgotten—you see, tomorrow I will be busy. Will you come for me the next day?"

"Yes, Memsahib. The morning after. As the sun rises."

Bill waited for me on the veranda. "Where in the world have you been? Oh, shopping." He answered the question himself, then added, "That's as lovely a piece of silk as I've seen. Where did you find something like that in Kataipur?"

I shrugged. "Honestly, I don't know if I could ever find the shop again or not. I'm exhausted; have you had tea?"

We sat down at a small table on the veranda away from a huddled group of tourists that I was surprised to see. "Somehow I didn't expect to find Kataipur on the tourist track." Anything to make conversation that wouldn't bring in Elizabeth.

"You don't generally. The old Maharaja is totally against it."

"That's what the guide at Darampur told me."

"These probably consider themselves lucky. Tourists always think of themselves as Marco Polos when they get to a place that's off the beaten path. Something new to talk about when they get home!"

I nodded, incapable at this point of keeping up a meaningless conversation, when he said suddenly, "Of course, it's lucky for us. . . ."

"It is?" I asked.

"Menon thought of it. He's a smart guy; worked for us a long time, and his father before him. We're going up into the mountain and get the statue, then weigh it in with their luggage to get it to Calcutta."

This was interesting. "Can you do that?"

Bill shrugged and grinned. "We'll know by this time next week." He changed the subject suddenly and his face lighted up. "Say, you should have been at the Pearl Ghat and you'd have seen something today. The pilgrims going to the Shiva Temple in the middle lake. Fantastic sight!"

I took a long breath before I dared speak. Had he seen me? Was that what he was working up to? "Oh?"

"Yes, it happens every Saturday, and they swarm around the dock like so many yellow wasps. Very colorful. I took some movies today. I'll show them to you and old man Sheridan when we get back."

I glanced at him from the corner of my eyes. What was he trying to say? After all, it really didn't matter if he had seen me. But it was irritating. The tea came and with it finger sandwiches and cake. Suddenly I was famished. I must have been eating as if I'd never see food again because Bill asked, "Bevan, dear, when did you eat last?"

I put a sandwich back on the plate self-consciously and offered it to him. "You know, I can't remember. I had a cup of coffee in the garden this morning, but I don't think I've eaten since yesterday. They do say fasting is good for the soul. I'll survive now until dinner."

"Eat up a storm then; we've a long night ahead."

I was beginning to regret my decision to go with Bill,

but didn't know how I could gracefully get out of it. So much had happened that I wanted to go to my room and lock the door, and give myself time to think on all the things Elizabeth had said. But would I have the stamina of character to say "Go away" should Park come knocking on my door? No. Better that I go to the mountains with Bill.

"—we'll take the lake boat and go across the Kalpa—"

"The Kalpa?" I asked, trying to concentrate on what Bill was saying.

"This lake of Kataipur. It means a measure of time. It was the old Maharaja's grandfather who dammed up the Moti and formed the string of lakes. They drop below each other, each fed from the one above, and dotted with small islands. There are crocodiles in them—but also very fine fish."

"I should think there would also be irrigation for the farmers."

"There's some," he said, "but mostly the maharajas were more interested in the palace gardens. The islands are picturesque."

"Have you been to any of them?"

"Oh, yes. They are lovely. Each lake has a few islands but the most spectacular ones are those in the second lake called the Stepping Stones to Heaven—Heaven being the Shiva Temple. It has the most glorious paintings and sculptures that I've ever found in one place—whole and intact. But one would have the devil's own time trying to spirit them away."

I didn't look at him when I asked, "Have you been there this trip?"

"No. I haven't really had the time. I don't want to go anyway when Prakash Vehta is around. He's poison so far as I'm concerned."

"I think so, too."

Bill looked up surprised. "Why would you think so? He's handsome, he's rich . . . I should think women would fall all over themselves for him."

The conversation was suddenly distasteful. I pushed my chair back to leave and just at that moment Park came out the door of the hotel and looked around. When he saw us he came directly to our table. I mumbled an introduction of sorts, my words stumbling over themselves. "You know Bill Holmes, Park Vehta. . . ." The men made no move to shake hands. They nodded coolly.

Then Park turned to me. "Since this is my anniversary, I've ordered dinner in my apartment tonight. A few friends from Delhi are here; I'll expect you at seven-thirty." He gave me a piercing, intimate look and added, "Wear something long."

A knot formed in my throat and rode down to my stomach and seemed to sink there into a permanent piece of marble. Finally I found the strength from somewhere to answer lightly, "I'm sorry—terribly sorry—I'm busy this evening. I'm having dinner with Bill. But thanks. Nice of you to think of me. If you'll excuse me now. . . ."

Bill rose when I did, and it was hard to keep my eyes from seeking Park's. Instead I was overly effusive to Bill and walked around the table to take his arm.

Suddenly Park's chair tipped over with a crash and when I looked at him, I knew he'd done it on purpose. His eyes were dark and his jaw was tense. Perversely I felt my spirit soar. Could he—could he possibly be jealous? I beamed on Bill. " 'Bye, dear. See you at dinner," I said, and left an astonished Bill Holmes looking after me. I felt Park's eyes on me long after I was out of sight.

Dinner that night was a quiet affair. There was no one around to playact for. I'd dressed carefully in a long gold lamé shirtwaist that did things to my figure and the color of my eyes, and never failed to draw compliments. Somehow I'd thought that perhaps Park might come into the bar with his guests from Delhi. But he didn't, and as soon as Bill and I had finished dinner, we separated to dress for our adventure. I put on everything warm I could find and left my room again by way of the mulberry tree. I was getting as adept as Tarzan at swinging from branches. I slipped through the garden, bypassing the lighted veranda and the driveway, to the Kataipur road.

Menon was there with his horse and cart. "Good evening, Dr. Blakley. Are you ready to go up into the mountain?"

"Yes, Menon. I think it's exciting."

"It will be. The mountain folk are as different from the desert people as the eagle from the camel."

"I think you're prejudiced."

"I am, Memsahib. I am of the mountain folk. They see with the eye of an eagle and soar on the falcon's wing when they dance or drink or make love."

I settled back into the tonga carriage and waited for Bill. Menon wanted to talk, but my silence discouraged him. We waited and we waited, until he began to grow restless. "Menon, I'm going back to the hotel to see what's keeping Mr. Holmes. If he comes while I'm gone, then go ahead—I know you're in a hurry to get started."

"Yes, it's a long way."

I climbed out of the carriage and hurried up the driveway. The doorman was leaning against a lamp post when I rushed up and if he was surprised to see me coming from that direction, he hid it very well. "Have you seen Mr. Holmes?"

"No, Dr. Blakley. Not since dinner when you were with him."

"That's strange. I was to meet him in the garden."
He looked at my odd assortment of clothes, then gave me
a sly grin and winked. "He'll be waiting, Memsahib. . . ."

The wink and smile were very clear. That anyone,
even a doorman, would think I had a rendezvous with
Bill Holmes annoyed me.

I asked at the desk, but no one had seen him since
dinner. "I'll check his room, then." I asked where it was
and the clerk told me. It was in the opposite wing to mine,
and when I reached it, my heart turned over. It was directly
across the hall from Park's apartment. I could hear music
and laughter coming from there, and light from the high
transom made a sharp bright rectangle on the ceiling. I
knocked on Bill's door softly at first, afraid someone from
Park's party would hear. There was no answer. I tried the
knob; it turned easily and I pushed the door open. It was
dark and I reached inside for the light switch. The first
I flicked turned on an overhead fan. I found the other
switch and, from the ceiling, light flooded the room.

I stepped inside calling softly, "Bill? Bill, where are
you?"

Then I saw the back of his head showing a little above
a wingbacked chair that faced a fireplace. I was surprised.
"Bill, for heaven's sake, Menon is waiting—what are you
doing?" He didn't move. I walked around the chair and
my breath surged out of me like a pumped bellows.

He was sitting straight up, the bit of slant of the chair
and the wings bracing him. His hair was combed carefully to one side, hiding the bald spot, and his eyes were
wide open—wider than I ever remembered seeing them,
and they looked like china-blue marbles. His mouth had
dropped open a little and his face, which had always been
as round and smooth and unlined as a baby's and as incredibly innocent, now sagged with loosened muscles.

Slack jowls drooped over the blue and pink ascot tucked in at his throat. He had on the navy checkered sport coat he'd worn to dinner.

Then I saw the dagger and recognized it. Both his hands were clasped around the hilt and I noticed for the thousandth time how pudgy and square and ugly they were. Now I stared at them and at the thin stream of blood that looked like a jagged shadow of the dagger. It cut an uneven design down his pale blue shirt and disappeared into the dark trousers he was wearing.

I stood looking at him for an eternity, taking in every detail. The dagger was a Deccan *Katar*—My God! *Identical to mine.* It must be—it had to be the same one that killed Jai.

I stared at it, unbelieving. Here was the mate to my dagger partially buried in Bill's chest. I saw the vivid chevron stripes across the wootz blade. I saw the cabochon rubies that edged the golden tiger's head protruding from Bill's knotted fists. And then I screamed. I screamed and ran from the room pounding on the door across the hall that was Park's. When he opened the door I could only look at him with stricken eyes and mutter, "Bill—Bill's dead—murdered. . . ." And I pointed across the hall.

I don't remember much about the rest of the evening. I never did think to send someone to tell Menon that we wouldn't be going to the mountains. But he must have gotten word because later I saw him in the hotel lobby. Park gave me something to drink, and when I woke up it was day and I was in my own room with the blinds pulled.

I sat up quickly, but a foggy dizziness ran through my head and I lay back, trying to work my thoughts into the right continuity. Suddenly they fell into place, and I thought my head would burst. Bill was dead. Someone had killed him with the Deccan *Katar* that was the match to mine. *The same one that killed Jai Vehta*—the one Elizabeth had found in her hand when she came to herself standing over her husband, watching him die. I shuddered and lay back, pulling the covers up over my shoulder. A deadening lethargy came over me and I felt I would never move again. Then the drug must have had a second round of effect because I went back to sleep. When I awoke, Park was standing beside my bed.

"Oh, no. Go away—" And I turned my face into the pillow.

He leaned over the bed. "Bevan, you have to get up. There's an official inquiry beginning. They want you there."

The nearness of him smothered me, and when I looked at him his eyes were grim.

"You drugged me last night," I said slowly.

"You had to sleep." His mouth was tense and he looked angry as he had the first time I'd seen him at the University Museum when he was hunched over the display case that held my dagger. But I had to know. "Did you . . . did you put me to bed?"

"Yes."

"Did you—did you—" I choked trying to express my thought. "Did you—?"

"No."

Suddenly I knew that he'd forgotten the night we spent together. I looked at him and never felt so alone. He was thinking of Bill, and I should be too. "Do you know who killed him?" I asked.

"It's pretty evident it was suicide."

I sat up quickly. "I'll never believe that—"

"He'd stolen the Deccan *Katar*. Someone had spirited it out of the palace." He walked to the door and opened it, then turned around and said slowly, "You couldn't be

satisfied with one, could you? You had to have them both."
The look we exchanged was a long one, and the only thing
I could read in his eyes was bitterness. "They are waiting
in the office behind the lobby. Don't be long." He closed
the door behind him.

Mechanically I pushed myself out of the bed on miserable, unsteady legs. I needed a cold shower to clear my
head. What was Park thinking? Where would he get the
idea that Bill had stolen the Dagger? That I wanted it?
Did he know it was the same one that had killed Jai?

Then I stopped cold, my hand on the bathroom door.
I shriveled into a knot and my legs crumpled. I leaned
against the wall supporting myself and my mind buckled
at the full surge of knowledge that flowed into it. It was
crystal clear—God, how clear! Park had killed Jai. This
man I loved—Elizabeth had called him a monster—had
killed his nephew and framed Elizabeth. Now he had
killed Bill Holmes with the same dagger and was blaming
me. Me—except for some reason he was calling it suicide.

chapter VIII

I walked into a group of strangers sitting around a table. Menon and Park were the only persons I knew. I refused to look at Park. He pulled out a chair as he introduced me, but I caught only quick syllables of unfamiliar names. I was in complete control of myself. From somewhere I had found a reservoir of strength. I lighted a cigarette and eyed the men coolly.

Just how, I wondered, would Park convince them that Bill had committed suicide? He interrupted my thoughts, asking me to tell the gentlemen who were investigating the death of the American, Bill Holmes, just what I'd seen when I opened the door to his room.

"The room was dark," I said in a strong, even voice. "I knocked first, and then tried the door. It wasn't locked. I turned on the light and walked in." One of the men interrupted. "Dr. Blakley, did you have an appointment with Mr. Holmes?" I nodded.

"A—how do you say in America—a date?" he asked. I

glanced at him with a half-smile, ignoring Park. Better a date than to admit an assignation with smugglers in the mountains. I nodded again.

"And he didn't keep this date?"

"No."

"Menon was to take you to Kataipur?"

I looked at Menon and nodded. "Yes, we were to meet him on the Kataipur road."

"That is strange, Dr. Blakley, that you wouldn't have Menon come to pick you up here at the hotel. Why the Kataipur road?" His voice was plainly suspicious, and I wondered if this was how Park was going to pin a murder on me. Perhaps I should tell everything I knew. I looked at Menon, but his eyes stopped me. "I like to walk. Exercise, you know."

"Still I do find it strange that you and Mr. Holmes, longtime friends that you were, would want to meet separately like that—I do indeed. Unless—" he hesitated and then looked at me with unfriendly eyes, "unless you had something to hide."

So it was to be blamed on me. I met Park's eyes then and knew there was nothing but pure hate in mine. "I have nothing to hide," I said. "I am here to see about any antiquities that I can buy for Midwestern University, and because I was in the neighborhood, so to speak, I have tried to search out Jai Vehta's wife, Elizabeth, whom I knew in America. If any of you can help me there, I'll appreciate it."

At the mention of Elizabeth's name the tension in the room grew. No one spoke. Finally my interrogator said, "Will you tell us what you found when you entered Mr. Holmes' room?"

"He was sitting in the wingback chair by the fireplace. I could see his head and thought he must be asleep. Of

course, when I saw him I was—I was dreadfully shocked."
I took a deep breath, stubbed out the cigarette, and defiantly looked each of them in the eye.

"It's very clear, you know, that Mr. Holmes committed suicide."

The impact of his statement was a surprise even though I had been partially prepared for it. So I wasn't to be thrown to the wolves on a trumped-up charge of murder, like Elizabeth. What then were his plans for me? I felt like a pawn on a chessboard waiting for the next move. When the silence grew so heavy that it bore down on me, I said, "That, then, is the conclusion you've reached?"

"Yes. We've sent a cable to that effect to his employer, Mr. Corraway Sheridan. We're shipping his body to America. You will accompany it back to the States."

I nodded. It was very smoothly done. Park had cleared the chessboard. This way he got rid of both of us. Well, God knows nothing would please me more than to leave this place—even if the price was Bill's poor murdered body, officially classified a suicide. "Then you are finished with me?"

The men rose and bowed slightly. "Yes" the spokesman said, "and we want you to know that we appreciate your cooperation at this sad time. I know it is a shock for you who knew Mr. Holmes so well. But there are events in the lives of others which we can neither understand, nor determine, nor interpret. My sincere sympathies, Dr. Blakley, to you and Mr. Sheridan. We will help in every way possible. A plane will meet you in Darampur tomorrow afternoon to take you to Delhi and we have reservations for you on Air-India to New York."

My eyes circled the table again and I didn't answer. I walked to the door. Park was there before me and opened

--•€{ 138 }€•--

it. The uppermost thought in my mind was to get away.

I hurried to my room to pack. I flung my suitcase on the bed, choking back tears. How could he—how could he! I had emptied my closet when I started to fold the cotton dress I'd worn to the island temple. I felt the bulge in the pocket and drew out the crushed and withered marigold. Elizabeth—I'd forgotten! I knew I had to go. I had to do this final thing for her. I looked at my watch. It was two o'clock. If I hurried, if I could find a gharry— night comes early in the mountains.

I dressed warmly and ran downstairs, glad to have something to fill the rest of the day. There was no one around, not even the doorman. Perhaps if I went to the road I could catch a ride on a bullock cart—anything to get Elizabeth's flower to the shrine. It had to be important to her, and if that was the last thing I could do for her, then it must be done. I wondered who would tell her I'd returned to the States. Would the old sadhu send word? Would she feel that I'd deserted her?

I had hardly reached the road when I saw the same gharry and the same snaggletoothed driver I'd had when I went to the dock. *Jamel was waiting for me!* I climbed in without as much curiosity as I'd have felt two days before. The intuitive feel of India is beyond understanding.

He snapped the reins with authority and we took off at a brisk trot. Red and yellow tassels bounced and bells tinkled from the harness at the steady clop of the hooves. I braced myself in the corner and held onto the wooden framework of the little awning, gazing out at the retreating gardens of the Moti Palace, at the dusty road fringed with trees, and thought, *This time tomorrow I'll be on my way to Delhi with a casket—Bill's. Then an overnight flight to New York, and from halfway around the world I'll be coming home to the university, to Corraway*

Sheridan, the collection—and instead of feeling relieved, I felt a strange dryness that shriveled the inside of me.

It had been such a short time ago I'd sat in front of Corraway Sheridan's fire and heard him say, *Bevan, it's time you got married.* And his threat, *Someday you'll be stunned by a bolt of lightning and a thunderclap, then go hog-wild over some guy who can tie you in knots*—there was something else he'd said—*And make you like it.* What was it about India that made some who had a feeling for the place prophesy, and others read minds and intentions before you yourself were aware of them? How could he have known that I'd—that I'd go hog-wild over a Hindu named Park. Certainly a thunderclap and a bolt of lightning had struck me with such force I'd never recover. I had given myself to a man who had used me until he had no further need for me. And now I was being sent away. Just like that.

It wasn't in my makeup to conform in any way to a slave syndrome. I had always been my own woman: Bevan Blakley, Ph.D., Phi Beta Kappa, recognized authority on oriental art, specialist authority on Indian art and philosophy, lecturer, authenticator, restorer, author. And now I was all these reduced to a snivelling, hypocritical sham of a liberated female, all because of a man I—I hated and I loved. And how can you equate the two and not lose your mind? A miserable emptiness wilted my newfound strength.

I pulled the faded marigold from the envelope and looked at it again, wondering what it meant.

There was little traffic on the road, and we turned down a small track to bypass the town. Then the trail turned into the rugged foothills and we circled around above Kataipur, losing sight of the village quickly as we passed into the forest area of the upper hills. The air was fresh and cool, redolent with a heady mixture of pine and fir and finely trampled dust the horse kicked up from the narrow road. My head felt lighter and the weight of my own problems seemed to lessen. I thought more and more of Elizabeth. How could I go off and leave her when she'd asked me to stay?

We passed a few pilgrims coming from the shrine. The track rose in easy stages higher and higher. Occasionally we met peasants coming down with baskets of wood balanced on short poles across their shoulders, or bent double from the massive load of twigs on their backs.

We crossed rude log bridges over streams that tumbled icy clear from the Himalayan snows to meet the Pearl. Giant ferns grew along the road, their fronds gray from the dust of pilgrims' feet. Jamel reined the horse into a dusty area edged with rocks and firs and ferns and helped me down. Then he led the way through the thick grove of trees to where steps had been cut into the rocks. Further on, we crossed a small swinging bridge over a deep ravine, and the roar of the snow water rushed up to me. The path was covered with a carpet of pine needles so thick that neither hooves from sacrificial animals nor pilgrims' feet could disturb it. We circled around a vast outcropping of rock and there was the Kali shrine.

The shrine had been cut out of stone to a height of about six feet, a square uncovered room roofed with pines and firs. Above, barely visible through the trunks of the trees, I could see the temple. A young boy wearing a dhoti and white shirt sat cross-legged on a stone wall with several earthenware plates beside him. I gave him rupees two for a plate and carried it to the shrine.

On it was a small unleavened cake made of ghee and rice flour, two small cups that contained spices and ghee, a tiny clay thimble filled with orange powder, a bright yellow marigold, and two short lengths of red and yellow ribbon. I took the envelope from my purse, broke it open, and added the withered marigold to the offering. A priest was standing by the swinging wrought-iron gates in front of the altar. He was dressed like the lad in a homespun dhoti and shirt which had ugly stains that no amount of sun-bleaching would erase. I knew very well that they were from animal sacrifices made the day before. The smell of blood lay heavy in the air.

On either wall of the shrine were tiled portraits of the Hindu deities Vishnu, Krishna, Shiva, Ganesh, Lakshmi, and others. Centered above the altar was the black goddess Kali. She was bedecked with red and yellow ribbons and garlands of marigolds, most of them shriveled now into brown buttons.

A fire burned at her feet and on either side were images of Shiva the Destroyer and Brahma the Creator. The priest took the plate, then kneeled in front of the fire chanting Sanskrit prayers. Occasionally he touched a rope that pealed bells strung through the trees. Then he threw the ghee—clarified butter—into the fire, with a small cup of water and the spices which symbolized the purification of air, water and food. The fire hissed and spit like a living thing, and a dark spiral of smoke curled up in front of the goddess Kali's face to blend with the overhanging evergreen branches. He took Elizabeth's small withered marigold from the plate, sprinkled it with holy water, then placed it reverently in the center of the still hissing blaze. The fire flared briefly, and unconsciously I bowed my head and breathed a prayer for Elizabeth—I had no idea to whom I prayed. At that moment, God, in the form of a Hebrew protector, a Christian Jesus, Vishnu or Shiva or Allah or Buddha was one—a Supreme Being with control over the affairs of men and concerned somehow with

Elizabeth Vehta and Bevan Blakley and our multitude of problems.

The priest stood then and came back to where I waited at the gate. He draped a mala of small white mountain flowers around my neck and the two ribbons of orange and red that had been consecrated with the other things. Dipping his finger into the clay pot of orange powder, he placed a tilak between my brows. He took the rice cake and the marigold, folded them inside a large leaf, and returned the packet to me. Afterward, I handed the priest rupees ten and he gave me an unexpected obeisance which I returned.

I mounted the steps slowly to the temple above the shrine. The way was outlined with bells, large brass ones with lovely incised decorations that gave out deep somber rings, to graduated smaller ones which tinkled as merrily as a child's rattle. And when I pulled the cord that connected them, the sounds boomed and tinkled and reverberated through the forest until I felt the very presence of —a god? A spirit? Any god. Any spirit.

I followed the sound of the bells through the wilderness of trees to the temple. Several pilgrims were there. I left my shoes at the flagstoned entrance and walked into the sanctuary. The wall had a six-foot, intricately designed and executed mosaic border above a marble wainscoting that told the story of the *Ramayana*—of Rama and Sita and the monkey-god Hanuman who saved her from the demon Ravana and was blessed by the Lord himself with eternal life—a visual Ram-Lila. The final panel in the series showed the Hill of God with an elliptical temple surrounded by yellow-faced monkeys with endless tails.

The opposite wall had a panel of Ganesh, the little potbellied elephant-headed god of wisdom and good luck, and told how he came by his blue elephant head. Parvati, his mother, was taking a bath and asked her son to guard the door. When Ganesh opposed his father's entrance, the Lord Shiva violently struck off his son's head. Overwhelmed by grief at what he'd done in anger, Shiva promised to replace it with the head of the first creature that passed—which was an elephant.

Along the back wall were panels of Krishna, his face blue as always, first as a youth cavorting with the milkmaids, and then his marriage with Rudmimi, and many of his battles with the forces of evil. The final panel showed his death, an accident, when a hunter mistook him for a deer and shot him in the heel as he sat under a fig tree in meditation. The hunter, recognizing Krishna, begged forgiveness from the dying god—Vishnu's ninth incarnation—and it was granted.

Over the altar, where candles framed her and she glowed with an iridescent luster, was the goddess to whom the temple was dedicated, the black goddess Kali, carved from fluid translucent obsidian. She was life-size, and the striking pinpoints of a hundred or more candles on either side gave her a feeling of life that I'd seen only once before in a carved statue—when the firelight played on the Emerald Kali and the imperfections in the stone made it a living thing. When Corraway Sheridan and I had looked at it, we both had felt its magic. A special gift indeed when a sculptor can give life to an inanimate mass. And I knew that the artist who had created this life-sized goddess from volcanic glass was the same one who carved the cabochon emerald. I wondered how it had escaped those buyers and sellers of sacred temple sculptures unless— that was it: It was simply too sacred, too frightening for any priest to bring himself to traffic with.

As I stood and looked at the statue, I knew that the

Emerald Kali belonged in this temple as surely as I knew a small boy had been sacrificed for her, and somehow I would get it back. I wondered if this priest in the white robe knew Pathak and his father, if he had somehow influenced the murder of the child. I wondered about the father and son. Were they still in the Delhi prison? I must inquire when we returned—I stopped. We. Bill and me. I was thinking of him in the present tense as though he were alive. Indian justice. A small boy is murdered. A middle-aged man is murdered. The son of a maharaja is murdered. And what happens? The father of the boy and the grand-father, too, should be placed in an institution for the insane. Bill's murder is whitewashed as a suicide. And Jai's? They found a patsy. A frame job neatly done on a gullible American girl who had only a deep love in her heart and no understanding of the Indian mind.

The gharry was waiting. Jamel was sitting under a tree absently scratching through the thick carpet of pine needles with a branch. "Ready now, Meesy?"

I took off the mala and laid it on the floor of the carriage with the leaf-wrapped package. "Yes." He helped me into the carriage as ceremoniously as a betel-stained, snaggle toothed driver could, and we clop-clopped back down the mountain, with the bells tinkling and the tassels dancing. The sun was gone and the twilight was brief, so that by the time we reached the hotel it was dark. I looked ahead as we came up the drive to the lighted veranda, half expecting Bill to appear and wave. Then I remembered. Would I ever think of him as dead? Probably not until I reached home and sat beside Uncle Coe at his memorial service in the University chapel.

I gave Jamel a handful of rupees, thanked him, and was almost to the terrace when he called to me and came running. He held the package and the mala. "Important you keep, Memsahib." I thanked him again, serious, unsmiling. There was no way the goddess Kali would let me forget her.

chapter IX

The tourists were settled comfortably in the bar when I looked in. Park, still with his guests from Delhi, was seated at a far table overlooking the garden. He caught my eye immediately, confirming the fact that he had been waiting, and pushed back his chair and started toward me. But I'd had enough this day. I turned and hurried across the hall and up the stairs. Tomorrow I'd be leaving. I'd never see him again and, even as I felt a certain pain, I thanked God it was so.

After I closed the door I leaned against it, out of breath. It had been a long day. I looked down at the packet in my hand looped with the mala of white flowers. What does one do with the residue of a Kali sacrifice?

I walked to the balcony and laid the package and the mala carefully on the balustrade. Perhaps the wind would blow it down to the garden and I'd be rid of it. I finished my packing, expecting to hear Park knock at my door any minute—I knew he would come to say good-bye—and I would be completely cool, completely self-composed, completely indifferent to him. In my fancy I had him begging my forgiveness—convincing me he had nothing to do with Bill's death or with Jai's. The dinner I ordered came and went. But there was no word from him. By midnight, I didn't know if I was glad or sorry. I did know that I was furious with myself because I let it keep me awake. Then came the pricking pang of conscience because I was leaving Elizabeth to face her Calvary alone. And Bill. Where was his body tonight? Was there anyone to keep vigil over it?

At some point I went to sleep and slept a thousand years—a deep dreamless sleep of utter exhaustion of brain and body, a sleep that gave neither my conscience nor my heart any quarter. And when I woke I was refreshed. I dressed, stacked my bags at the door, and was ready for breakfast.

There was no one else in the dining room; it was actually nearer lunch than breakfast, so I had my tray carried to the veranda. Park was there with his guests and when he invited me to join them, I did. After all, I decided, this would be the last time I'd see him, and if I wanted to rub salt in my wounds, it was my affair. He introduced me to a middle-aged man—something Kemor—in a Nehru cap and jacket, and his much younger wife who wore a blue sari and had black timid doe eyes and a gentle smile. He was something or other with the government.

I missed most of what Park said because the woman beside him captured my full attention. Her hair was coal black, braided into a knot at the nape of her neck, a heavy-scented gardenia fastened in it. She wore an apple green sari with a border of silver leaves, a string of pearls around her neck and small diamonds in her ears. She was without doubt the most beautiful woman I'd ever seen, and I could hardly take my eyes off her when her name seeped into my consciousness. Her name? Madhuri—Madhuri Jat. The breeze from the garden grew cold.

It was highly unlikely that there would be two Madhuris in Kataipur. And one of them I knew had been brought to Khilar Palace by Jai. It was in her apartment that he died.

This Madhuri had eyes only for Park. She had brushed hers over me insolently when Park introduced us—and then ignored me, speaking to the other woman in Hindi. I listened for awhile, but they talked only of clothes and movies. When Park's friend expressed his sorrow at Bill's death, I turned to him. We made desultory conversation about the weather until I finished my tea and croissant, then I asked to be excused. I wondered when I was supposed to leave for Darampur. As though my thought touched his, Park pushed back his chair and said abruptly, "Will you be ready to leave in an hour, Dr. Blakley?"

"Yes. I'll be ready." I nodded to the others and left. I'd have choked if I'd stayed another minute. This girl was the root of Elizabeth's problems, and very likely she had transferred her attentions from Jai to Park. Were they partners—in Jai's death?—Bill's?

As quickly as I thought of it I knew they weren't. Not in anyone's death. The girl was certainly interested in Park and suddenly I saw things clearly as a film washed from a mirror. My mind had twisted itself around an improbable fact and become lost in the maze. I knew as surely as I knew the sun rose in the east that Park was no murderer. And if he liked Madhuri, then she was innocent too.

He might want my Deccan *Katar* back; he might even

have thought I wanted the other one—but he wouldn't take me to his bed to get the one, nor would he kill to keep the other.

A strange peacefulness came to me as I walked up the steps to my room for the last time, as though a great burden had rolled from my shoulders. It was much better to leave in this frame of mind. I could tell Park good-bye with a smile and a casual handshake and never look back.

The room was empty, as sterile as though it had never been occupied. My bags were gone; the room had been cleaned. Ash trays were polished. The wicker waste-basket had been emptied and freshly lined with brown wrapping paper. Not a smidgen of dust. Blinds were drawn against the midday sun. I stood there a minute looking at the streaks of light that forced themselves through the blinds and like a seesaw my mind dipped again. That's the trouble with an intellectual, I thought, they can rationalize themselves out of any corner they're backed into.

All right, so Park didn't kill anyone. But someone had. And when I left, Elizabeth would be completely alone. I had to send help to her. Lane Thomas, perhaps.

I raised the blind and looked over the balcony to the mulberry tree. And I knew that I didn't want to leave. I wanted to stay. From somewhere inside me came an unreasonable yearning and I felt my roots reaching out tentatively, searching for a crevice, a stone—anything to attach themselves so they wouldn't be dislodged. I pushed open the door and stepped onto the balcony. The sun sifted through the leaves in warm speckles; the breeze was soft and fragrant. Wisps of smoke rose from the village, and I wondered if fresh flowers had been placed at the Kali shrine.

Then I saw the packet I'd left the evening before on the balustrade. It was all there, the ghee-rice cake, already making a grease mark on the marble railing, the wilted marigolds, the mala of white mountain flowers, shriveled now into a small brown string, the red and yellow ribbons. What had brought me back to find them? Why hadn't the cleaners thrown them away? Picking up the lot I leaned over the balustrade to drop them in the flower bed below. But I couldn't.

I carried them into the bedroom and dropped all of them in the wastebasket, then walked to the door, brushing the smell of the marigolds and the withered mala from my hands. At the door I stopped and looked back. I sighed. What the hell was the matter with me? I walked to the basket, retrieved each piece, the ghee cake, the ribbons, the mala, the marigolds, and wrapped them in the paper liner. Then I tucked it in the bottom of my shoulder bag.

Afterward I went to the desk, to pay my account and also Bill's. I asked for the key to check his room. The clerk told me that he himself had packed Mr. Holmes' things, and sent them with his body by truck to Darampur, but that I was welcome to look through his suite.

I unlocked Bill's door and closed it behind me. The room was as empty as mine had been, but I saw from the ash trays that it hadn't been cleaned. I picked up a stub. It was Bill's brand all right. There were no others in the tray. I'd read somewhere that was the first thing detectives looked for—a strange brand of cigarette, or one with lipstick. Dust and bits of charcoal were scattered on the hearth. The wing chair was gone.

Just then there was a knock on the door, and when I opened it, Menon was standing there. "Memsahib Doctor, I'm trying all morning to find you. I need to talk to you."

"Yes, come in, Menon. What is it?"

"It's the sculpture, Memsahib. It is in big trouble."

"Can I help? Do you need money?"

He nodded. "I will. Do you know about it?"

"Only that Mr. Holmes was having trouble getting it out."

"The temple statue is one of Shiva and Parvati—worth rupees a multimillion in the States. Mr. Sheridan had sent me five thousand dollars. But I need another five thousand now, and I think I can get it to Calcutta to the Orient Pak warehouse. It's going through with the tourists' luggage, and as a copy made in Nepal with a dealer's invoice from Katmandu—if their luggage is searched, which is unlikely."

I stared at him. "You mean it isn't from Nepal?"

"No. It's from the Kali Temple here. Bill went to Katmandu to get an invoice that would make the shipment legal. Most customs men don't know an original from a copy, and coming from Nepal they wouldn't question it. But the priest at the temple got—how you say?—cold feet after he sold it to Bill—when the little boy was killed. It's hidden in the mountains. I don't know where, but I can find the men who have it."

"Then by all means get it. I have the money for you." I looked at him, thinking—wanting to ask—still afraid to. "Menon," I said finally, "what do you know about Pathak, the Kali priest?"

"He was at the temple here long ago. He knew Mr. Sheridan, sold him many things—as I did, and my father also."

Of course, I'd always known that much Indian art was smuggled out of the country, and I don't think I had felt that it was wrong. They would be protected in the States—but then they belonged in their temples, didn't they? And for the first time the hard edge of my conscience turned on me. And all those things that Uncle Coe had—was that how he got the Emerald Kali? He said she'd been given to him. Now, suddenly, I didn't know who or what to believe. I sat down on the side of the bed and looked at Menon. "Have you ever heard of the Emerald Kali?"

"Yes, indeed, Memsahib! I never saw it. It was gone before my time, but my father knew about it."

"The priest Pathak sold it to Corraway Sheridan, didn't he?"

"No, Memsahib. The Rani Asha gave it to Mr. Sheridan."

I held my breath, then let it escape in a slow whistle. "How do you know this?"

"Everyone in Kataipur knows. Pathak the priest gave it to her. She, instead of making a palace shrine, gave it to the American."

"She still lives at the palace . . ." I said rather to myself. I remembered Elizabeth telling about the old Rani, the one who was educated and tried hard to hide it. She also said she'd not been out of the zenana for thirty years. How ever did she know Corraway Sheridan?

Menon stood before me, nodding his head. "Yes," he said, "she's in the zenana at Khilar. And has been in disgrace for many years."

"Why is that? Isn't she the mother of the three princes?"

"Oh, no. That is the youngest wife. The Rani Asha was his second wife. Her son was Prakash." If he heard my gasp he paid no attention. "But the Raja never believed that Prakash was his. So he bypassed him and made the other sons the legal heirs. He called him brother—"

"Menon!" I interrupted. "Do you know what you're saying?"

"Yes, Memsahib. My father told me. Is much gossip many years old—"

"I don't believe it!"

"Is true. I swear. And I tell you this. He would like to be Raja. He knows who he is. But I think maybe only Rani and Mr. Sheridan know for sure!"

"I'll never believe that. I've seen Prakash Vehta and Mr. Sheridan together—" I paused. I had seen them together in anger—and I knew now why Park had looked so familiar. It was his height. And that's where he got his strange-colored eyes—from his blue-eyed father. I felt sick. Suddenly I'd had enough of Menon standing there so free with his gossip. I opened my purse and pulled out some traveler's checks. Pay him off and be rid of him—

"Can you cash these here?"

"Yes, Memsahib. I'll see that the statue gets to Mr. Sheridan." He opened the door to go, then impulsively I called to him. "I don't understand how Mr. Sheridan could ever have an affair with the Rani when Hindu women are so protected."

"He was a friend of the Maharaja's. They knew each other well. And—somehow it happened. Good-bye, Memsahib."

"Good-bye, Menon."

Somehow it happened. Well, that took care of Park's sanctimonious theory on love and the Hindu woman! Women were the same all over the world when it came to love. But disproving his theory didn't make me feel any better.

With Menon gone, I checked the room thoroughly while my mind worked feverishly. *The sculpture was from the Kali temple!* So Park had been right. Bill had been smuggling out Indian treasures. And from the Kali shrine—Damn! He should have had better sense. The little boy dead—I wondered if Uncle Coe knew. Of course he didn't.

Then my mind boggled. Park—Uncle Coe's son! It didn't seem possible. But still. . . .

All the time I was opening drawers and closing them, looking in closets, feeling across closet shelves with no idea why I was searching.

Suddenly I saw it, and knew instantly it was what I was looking for. It was caught up next to the foot of a divan. A small rosette. It had fallen off something. What? A man's brocade tunic, the kind princes wear? A woman's cape? A sandal? I dropped it in my purse. I knew certainly that it hadn't come off anything that Bill Holmes wore. Even though his tastes were flamboyant, he'd never wear a brocade jacket with gold rosette buttons. Now all I had to do was find where it came from. But I'd never have the chance. I was leaving Kataipur in less than an hour. So the gold rosette would go back to America with me—and Bill's death would go unsolved.

I closed the door behind me and went down the steps to turn in the key. Park was waiting. Suddenly I was sorry I hadn't asked Menon about Madhuri—he seemed to know all the other scandal of the Pita-Singh family. Park walked with me to the car as his friends watched from the veranda. Singh, the chauffeur, opened the door for me and Park touched my elbow to help me in. It was almost enough to undo me. I'd be gone in two minutes. Gone forever. And in the palace limousine at least I'd be driving in some comfort back to Darampur. Not like the jolting, wheezing ride I'd had in the mail bus. Singh closed the door, but opened the one in front, and I was surprised when Park climbed in beside the chauffeur's seat. Why would he go with us to Darampur? Why? He didn't turn around and he didn't speak. Neither did I.

At first I sat stiffly in the middle of the back seat staring defiantly ahead between the two men. Before long, however, I relaxed in a corner and my eyes kept turning to the back of Park's head. For the first time I noticed a few gray hairs. I wondered if that was an inheritance from Corraway Sheridan. And I thought again of the resemblance between the two men. Was that what had made me think I'd known him before? What if—in that conjectural transmigratory theory of Hindu religion—I *had* known him before? Had he felt it too when he took me to his bed so easily as though we were husband and wife?

It had been that sort of thing. As natural as breathing in and breathing out, until—until he'd made it plain that it wasn't that way at all. That it had only been a pleasant interlude that he would have liked to continue the following night—perhaps as long as I was in Kataipur. One that he could terminate just as quickly as he'd snap his fingers. Had he substituted Madhuri for me the next night—and the next? And that bit of conversational fluff he'd thrown at me about Hindu women saving their precious gift for marriage. What about his Mother?

He must have felt my stare on the back of his head because he turned around and caught my eye before I had time to look out the window. But neither of us smiled and we both looked away quickly. We were approaching the town, and Singh flew through at a dangerous speed. Soon we were on the outskirts. I closed my eyes. There was a long, uncomfortable trip ahead, and the best thing I could do would be to block out Park's image and try to rest. Would I ever, ever wipe him from my mind? Would I ever, ever stop remembering the touch of him?

And so I curled into the back seat, resting my head against the padded corner of the limousine, closed my eyes and lost myself in pleasant daydreams of what might have been—

After some time, far too soon to be in Darampur, the car slowed. I opened my eyes, then sat in shocked and frightened silence. We were at the triple gates of Khilar Palace and had stopped to let an old man and his donkey get out of the way. A wave of complete terror soaked my skin with a cold sweat and it was a full minute before I could voice my question in a normal voice. I had to keep cool. He must not know, he must not even dream that I was frightened. I said coolly, very deliberately, "The resemblance of Darampur to Khilar Palace is remarkable. I hadn't noticed the other day."

"Your sarcasm is well taken. I should have told you our plans were changed."

"I'm sure I don't know why you should. Few people in Kataipur have any rights when their sovereign family acts."

The car passed through the gates and threaded its way along the compound as we talked. I sat rigid as a tent pole.

"Elizabeth wants you," he said. "I was afraid you'd refuse to come, and I couldn't give you any choice. She needs you."

"You're lying. Elizabeth is on the island. I've seen her."

"I know. My brother sent word that she was returned to the palace yesterday evening. She wants you with her. I sent my secretary to Darampur early this morning to escort Holmes' body to the States." He paused a minute as the limousine turned into the palace courtyard. Then, when I didn't answer, he continued, "I hope you'll be willing to stay—but it really doesn't matter. You will. She needs you."

I answered stiffly, "Of course I'm glad to help Elizabeth. But I'm an adult. A grown woman. I like to think I have the intelligence to decide these things myself."

"I have no faith in women's intelligence. They can only feel." His eyes were cold as a yellow-green glacier and I wanted to tear at him. To scratch his face, to pull his hair, to hit him, to hurt him some way—any way at all. His expression didn't change, and I knew he was reading my every thought and that was proof enough to him that his statement was true.

The limousine pulled up beside the elephant walk and Park jumped out almost before Singh had cut the motor. I looked around the courtyard. It was nearly empty. The uniformed guards stood at attention saluting Park. There was only a heavy humped bull browsing beneath the peepul tree where the old sadhu had sat on his small earthen platform. I wondered if the holy man knew that Elizabeth had been brought back to the palace.

I walked down the marble path and up the steps, staying as far as possible from Park. The door opened and I went inside, ignoring the *"Namaste"* of the turbaned bearer. "Highness, Memsahib—"

The great hall was empty. The splash of the fountain was the only sound. Opposite, the garden looked like a great rectangular painting with the sky and the lake fusing in a long stretch of horizon. I stood waiting, docile as any servant, to be led to Elizabeth. And I remembered the spider and the small iridescent bug. It had been a stupid bug to get caught in a spider's web in the first place. It had probably flown right back into the web—and to the waiting spider—as soon as I left.

chapter X

"Hunan will take you to Elizabeth. You will share her apartment." I didn't answer. But I turned dutifully and followed the bearer as he padded down the corridor. Park didn't say he'd see me again and I thought very likely he wouldn't. I'd be shut up in a zenana with Elizabeth and—what was it Elizabeth had said?—never see a man again? In spite of myself I smiled. Perhaps Park was right when he said women operated by feel and not intelligence. Could that also be intuition?

I followed the crested turban down the length of hall and up a narrow flight of steps, then into a foyer that opened onto a marble-screened balcony. Below me I could see the garden, lovely and silent. I felt the wind from the lake broken into drafty currents through the fretted screen. Crystal chandeliers as bright as diamonds hung along the balcony and moved faintly in the breeze.

Elizabeth came to meet me. She was wearing a white sari as usual, but her hair was knotted on her neck with a veni, a crescent of yellow jasmine. She looked beautiful as always, but her face was drawn and her eyes had dark circles under them. "Bevan, there's no way I can tell you how—how pleased I am to have you here. I hope it doesn't inconvenience you. They've promised me you'll have complete freedom to come and go as you wish."

I took her hand; it felt feverish and clammy. "I'm glad you wanted me, Elizabeth." There was no way that I could tell this bloated child that I'd been shanghaied and there was no chance that I'd be given any kind of freedom. "Why did the Maharaja bring you back?"

"They have reasons—for everything they do." Then she changed the subject. "Have you had lunch?" She clapped her hands and the old ayah, Leela, came in with a tray of sandwiches and tea. "In your honor we're having American food. See these sandwiches—pure chicken, and very good, too."

I wondered if the tea was drugged and then threw caution to the winds. I'd find out soon enough. Elizabeth didn't seem in such a vague state of mind as she had been when I saw her at the temple. But she didn't look well. "Elizabeth, when does the doctor say your baby is due?" I asked her over a second cup of tea.

She gave a short laugh. "I haven't seen a doctor since I've been in India."

"Not even since you've been pregnant?"

"It just isn't done here. Hindu women won't go to any but women doctors. And childbirth isn't thought to be that big a deal."

I was shocked. "Elizabeth, you're an intelligent woman. You know you need to be checked periodically by a doctor. Who's taking care of you?"

"Leela. She's very capable. She sees to the things I need."

"And who will deliver your baby?

"She will."

I stood up. "That's stupid. I'm going to see Park and ask for a doctor to be brought here from Delhi—or anywhere—immediately. There have to be some medical missionaries somewhere near."

"Please, Bevan. Don't make a stir. I'm all right—honestly!"

She had seemed terrified when I suggested going to Park. But I wouldn't give up easily. "You've got to be sensible about this. Your baby's life might depend on it."

"Believe me, Bevan, it's not that important. No woman in Khilar Palace ever had a baby delivered by a doctor. Childbirth is a perfectly normal thing. You stay in seclusion, have your baby, you're purified—it's very simple. Leela delivered Jai and she will deliver his son. Now quit worrying and let me show you my apartment. I love it, and I'm so glad to be back in it—not forced to live in the zenana. I—Jai and I—furnished it with things I found in Delhi."

I carried my cup and followed her through the foyer into the sitting room. There was a silky gold Isfahan on the floor with a design of cream-colored feathers and symmetrical traces of royal blue and a stylized border of amber square-cut fleurs-de-lis. It was the most beautiful rug I'd ever seen and looked as new as the day it had come off the loom. "Can you believe it's sixteenth century? It came with the quarters!"

"What wouldn't Corraway Sheridan give for *that!*"

She showed me the special things she and Jai had collected, the Rajput miniatures, the Chinese porcelains and tapestries, a collection of gold betel dishes, two dozen or more artifacts that made my mouth water. "You know, very few Indians are interested in collecting art. You go into the home, the average home, and you see some calendar art, a picture of Indira Gandhi and Lakshmi or Krishna or Ganesh, and that's all. It's rather pitiful."

"Let's hope you'll be the wave of the future—as a good Hindu—" And of course I was sorry as soon as I said it.

From the sitting room with its comfortable traditional furniture, through a double archway, was her bedroom. It was lush with silks, brocades, mirrors, furniture inlaid with chips of ivory, mosaic walls and floor with crisscross designs of black and green marble. A low bed was centered on a six-inch platform and silk netting was pulled to the ceiling in graceful swags. "Mosquitoes," Elizabeth said. "You've never seen such mosquitoes or so many. They spray the garden every morning, but still they come, so be sure and use your net." I remembered the garden that morning I'd come and the strange stillness of it. The smell of death—and that was all it had been. A gardener spraying for mosquitoes! My imagination had been working overtime that morning. Then I wondered—was it still?

A magnificent tiger skin hung over the mantle. When Elizabeth saw me looking at it she said, "Jai killed it himself when he was sixteen. I want the little Raja to have it."

"To wrap him in a tiger's skin—"

She laughed. "The Indian version of Bye-o Baby Bunting." And I wondered how she could have kept a sense of humor after all she'd been through—and still had to face. To one side of the bedroom was a cubicle with moorish arches and stained glass. There was a narrow cushioned ledge that circled it, and above—a velvet padded swing hung on gilt chains. "The most popular indoor sport of the maharajas!" I said, remembering the hundreds of Deccan and Rajput miniatures that showed the princes dillydallying with their favorites on a velvet swing. "The first time I've seen one, though."

"And please notice that this velvet nap is well worn! Not by me, however!" It was fun to laugh with Elizabeth, to be able to joke about the princes and their excesses.

The bathroom looked like a pavilion with a small sunken swimming pool. A peacock punka hung over it with a golden cord draped to one side. "And how about that," Elizabeth said, "sitting in your tub with your very own slave pulling a peacock fan?"

And I said, "Cleopatra used milk. What do you use?"

"Nothing but fresh cream and attar of roses. In the good old days all the water was brought in from the lake and it took quite an army of slaves to carry enough to fill that pool. But Jai's grandfather had water piped in. I don't know how pure it is; I quit worrying about things like that long ago."

We crossed the bath into my bedroom, a small, beautifully-furnished antechamber with a single bed in the shape of a swan inlaid with gold and silver, a tall narrow chest of drawers, a gold and silver wardrobe with a full-length mirror, all small and to scale in the little room. There was a strange sort of appendix attached that again was framed with moorish arches but filled in with bricks of Venetian glass in every conceivable color, blue, red, yellow, green, and all mixtures of in-between shades, roses and pinks and lavenders. There was a small knee-high bench with a velvet cushion. "What in the world," I asked, "is this?"

"Would you believe," she answered, "this is where the favorite of the moment came to amuse herself?"

"No, I can't. How do you mean amuse herself?"

"Since they couldn't read, their only diversion other than entertaining their prince was looking through the different panes of glass—seeing the garden and the lake and the sunset through the various colors. Exciting, no?"

We left the sad little cubicle and examined the balcony on the opposite side. There was a winding staircase that spiraled to the terrace below and continued its corkscrew twist overhead. "Where does that go?" I asked.

Elizabeth hesitated a second, then answered, "To the apartment above."

"Oh." I knew she meant Madhuri's.

She let a long sigh escape. "Yes, Madhuri. But she isn't here now. I don't know where they sent her. Back where she came from probably." I didn't tell her that I knew where she was—and that if Park had anything to do with it she'd probably be back. The bearer came with my luggage and Elizabeth helped me unpack. I was folding sweaters in a drawer when I saw the ring of keys in a corner. I pushed them to one side. Probably each room had its set for outside doors, closets, and wardrobes.

Afterward we walked in the garden. "This is unprecedented, you know. The zenana is that opposite wing there, and I can feel the eyes of every woman and child up there."

"Will I get to meet them?"

"I don't know. I really had no idea that you'd be allowed to come."

"How did you manage it?"

"I threatened to kill myself."

"Elizabeth!"

"It's true. And they knew it. After you came to the island, I decided I couldn't go through with it—just to be kept alive to furnish an old man his heir. Leela knew I meant it. I was going to throw myself over the balcony. She got word to the old Raja and he sent for me. For the first time since we married he talked to me. And, Bevan, he was very kind. We talked a long time. He told me he knew that I didn't kill Jai. . . . But that for my safety and that of the child someone must be with me constantly. Thank you—thank you for coming." She smiled and reached for my hand.

In spite of her sari and the thick bun at her neck with the veni of jasmine blossoms, and her thick body, she looked like the beautiful young girl I'd known at Midwestern University and an uncompromising twist wrenched my heart. "You don't suppose he'd let me send for Aunt Edith, do you? She'd get things straightened out here soon enough—" And even as I joked, I knew that if the Maharaja knew that Elizabeth hadn't killed Jai, then he knew who it was, and a spasm of fear made me shiver.

But Elizabeth didn't notice. She laughed and said, "Not Aunt Edith—can you imagine her here? But I must write her. Somehow, though, it's hard to do. How do you write your aunt that you've just been absolved of the murder of your husband and you're expecting momentarily to bear his child? You write her, Bevan."

"I will. I'll do it today." I wondered if the letter would ever be mailed. We walked through the garden paths aimlessly, until we reached the lake shore. Opposite were the pale hills, almost inseparable from the soft clouds that edged the horizon. The lake was as smooth as a mirror and reflected the hills and the clouds so that its far shore-line was blurred. Occasional fishing boats with small square sails sat like permanent decorations on the glassy blue surface. Lake Kalpa breathed quietly at our feet, in and out with soft bubbles when a stone or tree trunk broke its rhythm. We followed the shore line to an inlet that circled behind the wing of the palace where Elizabeth and I were staying. Here was a dock, a boathouse and a small motor launch with a pink awning bobbing beside it.

The inlet was fringed with trees and it was easy to see why the garden was invisible from the boat that took the pilgrims to the island. A kingfisher dived from a piling and brought a wriggling silver fish back to his perch. I turned my back. I was tired of identifying with the victims of nature.

We had dinner that night with the women in the zenana. I could feel the thick tension in the air as Elizabeth introduced me to the widows of Durga and Bhimi, to the old Maharani Asha, and to the younger wife, the mother of the boys now dead and the young daughters. The adults all wore white saris, the young girls bright ones of red and yellow. After their initial shyness with me, they chattered like magpies and I had difficulty keeping up with their conversation.

The matriarch, the Rani Asha, shriveled and wrinkled and brown, looked at me with black eyes and the shadow of a smile on her face. Was this little old lady truly Park's mother? She only nodded when Elizabeth introduced me to her, but she had a friendly air about her that was obviously lacking in the other adult occupants of the zenana.

Toward the end of the meal, when my eyes were damp from the hot chillies and my throat was burning like sin, she suddenly asked in perfect English, "You know Mr. Sheridan, I believe, Dr. Blakley?"

"Yes," I answered and looked at her swiftly, hoping to find a clue. "We are very good friends. You speak excellent English, Highness."

"I was educated in England and lived in Europe many years. My father was in the government service—and my husband."

I was overwhelmed with curiosity. How had this well-educated and charming woman ended up in a backwoods zenana? Perhaps Elizabeth would know. I was sorry when the meal came to an end and Elizabeth rose to go back to her apartment. I wanted very much to continue talking to this woman. "I'll see you again?" I asked.

"Yes," she answered, "tomorrow. Good night. It is very pleasant to have you here, Dr. Blakley."

"I wish you would call me Bevan. Somehow the "doctor" doesn't set well in India."

"I wish you were a medical doctor, B—Bevan." The name didn't come easy to her lips. "Elizabeth needs one."

I raised my eyebrows. Elizabeth had gone, only the Rani and I were at the door. "You think so too?"

"I know so."

"Then can't you do something about it? Talk to His Highness?"

"I haven't talked with my husband for thirty years."

I looked at her, shocked. "You haven't talked to him in thirty years? That's incredible!"

She smiled. "Yes, isn't it? But there have been compensations. I've helped raise the children, watched them grow, lived while they died, and now my great-nieces are my joy . . . and Elizabeth's baby. I'm very glad you are here."

I pressed her hand affectionately as I left. "Good night, Highness. Do you think we can walk in the garden tomorrow?"

"Only in mine—I'll send for you. Good night, Bevan."

There was little that Elizabeth could tell me about the Rani. She wasn't the Maharaja's first wife. He had buried two wives before he married her in Europe, and he was much older. She'd never had any children. Either she was barren or had incurred the Raja's disfavor. She had been in the zenana ever since she'd married and come to live in Khilar. And that was about thirty or so years ago. Soon after that the Raja married Jai's mother. But she never had the status in the zenana that the Rani Asha had, possibly because the Rani Asha had been a princess in her own right.

If Elizabeth had heard the gossip about Park and his parentage, she didn't want to mention it. I decided she hadn't. I wondered about the Rani's age. If she hadn't spoken to the Maharaja for thirty years—and she had been young when she married, say sixteen or under—she'd be forty-plus now. And she looked a hundred and ten. All except her eyes and they were young and alive. What had she meant when she said she could only walk in her own garden? I looked forward to seeing her the following day.

That night, after Elizabeth and I had returned to our apartment, I asked her about the Rani's garden. "It's the garden for the zenana," she answered. "It's rather unbelievable that such a lush place could grow two stories up. There are trees and fountains and birds—an altogether lovely place. The Rani keeps it herself, and if she has to have a gardener to do some pruning, she wears a veil and the other women stay out of sight. She's tended it for— well, ever since she married."

The Rani sent for us the next morning. We had coffee in her apartment, then she led us up several flights of steps to a marble cupola. We walked slowly so that it wasn't too hard on Elizabeth. "I want you to see the garden first from here."

And when I looked through the delicately carved moorish arch, I was amazed. Spectacular is not a strong enough word for the garden that lay beneath us. I had never seen anything like it. It was secluded in an inner courtyard and divided into three sections. Each of the end gardens were exactly alike, centered with marble fountains. There were perfectly sized orange trees in great tubs at the four corners of the garden. A crystal stream came from somewhere, divided around the center garden, came together again in the third, and then disappeared. Graceful humpbacked bridges spanned it at intervals. Glossy flowering creepers vied with the clinging ivy to cover the walls. But it was the center section that held my attention. The flower beds were patterned like a Persian rug. Narrow paths followed the stylized curves of the brilliant symmetrical groupings of red and yellow and blue flowers. Black-leafed ferns defined its border and at each corner was a perfectly round pomegranate tree heavy with red fruit. White peacocks and their hens strolled aimlessly through the garden, white doves flitted about, and fancy fantail pigeons, all white, strutted along the walks.

I was speechless. Elizabeth said, "I'm glad you saw it from up here first. It's hard to get the proper perspective when you're in the midst of it."

Finally I found my voice. "Did you—did you do all this?" I asked the Rani.

"Oh, no. It's been here a hundred years or more. But I've loved it. You'll notice there are only white birds in the garden. The Maharaja's grandfather placed them in the garden when his favorite wife died, and these are their descendants. Of course, all kinds of birds join them at different times. But these stay."

From our tower we could see in all directions. The town of Kataipur far to the left snuggled around the Kalpa, then came the other two lakes and the island temple. Almost beneath us was the village of Khilar, to our right was the old fort and the extensive buildings of the palace that followed the curve of the lake. "Those are the elephant stables. The mahouts are there beneath the trees playing cards. I wish you could see them when they're on parade. Next week is Diwali, but the festival, of course, won't be celebrated this year."

I started to ask why and stopped quickly, remembering, of course, that the palace was still in mourning for Jai.

Down in the garden it was as exquisite as the bird's-eye view had been. We entered through a Chinese moon gate covered with a cascade of blue morning glories. The air was fragrant with jasmine and roses, and built into the wall by the gate was a charming garden shrine to Lakshmi. She was holding a lotus blossom and standing on another above the curling waves of the churning ocean. It reminded me of Venus rising from the sea in an iridescent shell. The statue of the goddess of love convinced me again, if I had ever doubted, that the Hindu religion also had a long tap root into the Mediterranean area.

We spent most of the day there. The little girls came into the garden to play and chase butterflies, then had their lessons with an old priest who taught them Sanskrit chants and read to them from the *Ramayana* and the *Bhagavad-Gita,* while their mothers embroidered lengths of linen with wool thread. Their work was beautiful and much like the crewel I'd bought in Delhi.

I felt awkward in my pants suit with these women of the zenana and wished I had a sari besides the saffron one I'd worn to the temple. I think the Maharani Asha read my mind because when Elizabeth and I returned to our apartment Leela brought me half a dozen lovely saris from the Rani. They were of every color and in silks and cottons and woolens so fine they could be pulled through a ring. And with them she brought some velvet slippers in red and blue and yellow. "These are the Rani's, too," she said. "They should fit. She has a very long and narrow foot, and noticed that you have too."

They did fit. Then Leela and Elizabeth draped me in the saris and I loved them. It was like a fashion show, and wearing them, I felt a kinship with all the women at

Khilar, but especially with the Rani Asha. I felt another root reach out tentatively, timidly, wanting to encircle this woman's heart. After that I wore saris constantly.

The days passed. When Elizabeth and I weren't in the zenana, we sat in the palace garden. We learned to embroider with Leela standing over us laughing at our awkward stitches. I wrote letters to Uncle Coe, to Edith Dameron, and to Lane Thomas, and knew with a certainty that they never left the palace. Old Deleep with the strange half-eyes looked after us. I got to know the servants and call them by name. I became friends with the young girls, though not with their mothers.

And every day we'd see the cobra. He seemed to want company. At first Elizabeth and I were frightened of him, but when we watched the servants talk to him and feed him milk in a small brass bowl, call him Naja-Naja and stroke him with a pigeon feather when he struck his pose and flared his hood, we decided he wasn't all bad. He must surely have been provoked to have struck the small boy, Krishna. We even began to form a certain attachment for him. "Does he ever go in the palace?" I asked one day.

"Probably. The doors are always open. And I'm sure that in all the old forts and palaces there are cobras in the walls and basements. They live forever, I think."

"But you don't know where this one stays?"

"No," Elizabeth answered. "I hadn't thought about it. Until just lately, I'd not get that close to him."

So the days and the nights passed in monotonous regularity. The moon grew full and waned. The stars moved in their orbits across the sky. Diwali came and went with millions of lights all over India, and thousands in their wee clay saucers set along the parapet of the palace roof winking like so many stars until their wicks soaked up all the mustard oil and died.

It was difficult now for Elizabeth to climb stairs, so we seldom went to the zenana. We talked and talked and talked. She never grew tired of hearing about her classmates at the university, her old professors, everything that I could remember to tell.

Then one morning Deleep came to us as we sat in the garden. "His Highness wishes to see Dr. Blakley."

I hesitated, then looked at Elizabeth. "I thought I was supposed to be with you every minute—"

"That's all right. I'll stay here until you come back." So I followed Deleep through the central hall, the first time I'd been there since I'd arrived, and down another of its sunburst corridors to the lavishly decorated audience room with the famous ivory throne at the far end. Deleep hardly gave me time to look around before he led me through a door with an armed soldier standing at attention. Inside, a servant was waiting. "Tell His Highness the American woman is here," he ordered in Hindi.

We followed him through a maze of rooms in the royal apartment until we came to the bedroom. The Maharaja was lost in the great canopied gilt bed and looked like a small brown turtle peeking out from the oversized sheet. He was propped up with pillows and wore a silk turban with the royal cockade and the eye of a peacock feather. He was so old and shriveled and dried it seemed that a breath of air would blow him away.

Deleep said, "Dr. Blakley, Highness."

I curtsied with my palms together and whispered, "*Namaste,* Your Highness." His eyes were narrow slits with tiny specks of white showing occasionally as his pupils darted back and forth like an animal at bay. He gave a slight indication of nodding, then Deleep left and we were alone, the old Maharaja and I.

His voice was as weak as an autumn leaf and that's

what he reminded me of. A gorgeously colored leaf waiting for that final breeze to blow him away. He was cleanshaven; his skin was a mass of crosshatch wrinkles. He wore a blue brocade jacket embroidered with red and gold. He meant to go in style, this patriarchal old man. After Deleep left, he stared at me for a minute or more with eyes that blinked and watered, but he never took them off my face. At last, when I decided I couldn't stand another second of his silence, he said, "You look very Indian." His voice was frail, mostly labored breath, a barely audible whisper, and he spoke in perfect English.

I smiled. "Yes, Highness, I love the saris. They make all Hindu women kin."

"But you are not Hindu."

"I know. But there is a bond."

"There is?"

I didn't answer because I didn't know what to say. What was the bond? If I couldn't explain it to myself, how could I answer this old Raja? Was it Park? Not really. I kept an artificial smile on my face, and he asked, "You have seen the Rani Asha?"

"Yes, Highness. A charming woman."

"But very old."

Very old! Compared to this old man? Hardly, but I decided my guess that she was in her forties was many years off. Then he asked, "The Lady Elizabeth, she is all right?"

"I think so, Highness. Of course, she should have a doctor."

Again the old man lay without speaking for a long time. Suddenly he said, "Tell Deleep to come."

I walked to the door and, in Hindi, asked the bearer to call Deleep, then went back to the old Raja's bedside. He hadn't paid the slightest attention to my request for a doctor for Elizabeth. Deleep was there almost by the time I was. He entered from another door and I was quite sure he'd been listening—but what really had he overheard? Even if he could understand the faint whispering from his ruler. I listened to the Raja order, "Have the Rani Asha come."

Surprise registered in Deleep's serpentine eyes. "Yes, Highness."

I stood there uncomfortably shifting my weight first to one foot and then the other. The old man lay back with his eyes closed. After an interminable time there was a knock on the door and it opened. Deleep stood back to let the Rani Asha enter. She walked to the bed with easy grace, bowed with her palms together. "I am here," she said.

He stared at her for so long that I began to feel uncomfortable. Then a slow flush began to work its way from her neck over her face, and she dropped her eyes so that I could see only a half moon of dark lashes. Then as quickly as she blushed, the color faded and she became deathly pale. Still the Maharaja said nothing. Neither did Deleep. Finally the old Raja raised one hand weakly and motioned to the door, then closed his eyes. Deleep herded us both out of the room, through the chain of rooms to the throne room, and then the Rani Asha and I separated. She took my hand, held it for a minute and lifted it to her cheek. Her eyes searched mine, curiously pleading—and I couldn't understand why. She turned without saying good-bye. I felt a heaviness upon my heart that made me take a deep breath to try to dissipate it.

I didn't see the Maharaja again. One day I was in the garden with Elizabeth when Park joined us. He sat for a few minutes, but it was a strain on the three of us.

When he left, he kissed Elizabeth's hand. "Princess, I wish you the best of luck."

And she answered coldly, "As long as you are here, I shall need it."

It stung me as much as it did him. I saw the quick flash of pain in his eyes. I could hardly bear it. She had no right. Afterward when I spoke to her about it she said, "Bevan, you don't know that man. He's cruel, vindictive. I know he's the one the Raja meant when he said he knew who killed Jai. Don't waste any sympathy on that man. . . ."

Still the days passed and Elizabeth grew larger and larger with no sign of delivering. I would have given half my life for a doctor. Then one day, bored while Elizabeth napped, I walked into the main hall from the garden to feed the goldfish some leftover crumbs. Suddenly I stopped.

I had seen Madhuri Jat. She was crossing the hall from Deleep's office to a corridor I'd never been down— and she walked with the assurance of one who belonged. I knew well enough that she had not just arrived. As quickly as that she was out of sight and I ran across the hall watching as she turned to the right. I hurried after, hearing the swish of her sari and her sandaled feet as she rushed ahead of me up another corkscrew stair.

I stopped then. Did I want to pursue her? Well, no. Although there was everything against her in my mind— she and Jai; she and Park— Did those steps lead to the apartment above Elizabeth's? I'd never suggested that we go there. That had seemed a bit much to ask of her. But I'd like to go. I wondered why Park brought her back? Of course, the answer to that was simple enough. But how could he be so insensitive?

It was the morning after I discovered Madhuri that

I became sick. It flashed through my mind I'd been poisoned—and that Madhuri had to be the reason. Certainly she knew I was here.

Leela took care of me, and Elizabeth bathed my forehead with cold water, and I turned inside out. The rest of that day I stayed in my room, content to watch the play of light on the ceiling from the colored bricks, wishing I was home.

It was well over a month I'd been in the palace with Elizabeth. The Rani Asha didn't call for either of us to visit her again and I missed that. I hadn't seen her since we'd stood around the old Raja's bed and he had looked at his wife and not spoken. Just looked, and it had devastated her. I continued to be ill, but it wasn't as bad as the first time and I was careful of what I ate.

Then one evening when I felt better, I decided I'd call on Madhuri. Elizabeth had gone to bed early—she seemed to sleep so much lately, and I didn't know if that was good or bad. I went up the spiral stairway to a brass-studded door and knocked. No one answered. I tried it, but it was locked. Remembering the set of keys in the chest of drawers, I returned for them. There was a big brass one that might just possibly—

It did. I turned the key slowly and pushed. The door opened into a small dark foyer with a lighted filigree lamp hung high in the ceiling. Shadows were blurred and diffused in all directions. I tiptoed to the door and looked into a sitting room almost the twin of Elizabeth's, except it was carelessly furnished. Certainly the apartment was occupied. There was a lingering scent of perfume—gardenia. I'd never liked it. It was too strong and it always irritated me that anyone would wear it. Now it almost nauseated me.

I knocked again softly before I entered. If Madhuri

came, I'd simply plead innocence, and that—curious about the old palace—I was exploring. But no one was there. It was plainly hers. A garland of gardenias hung over the portrait of some turbaned prince and the odor was sickeningly strong. There was a permanence about the room, and I knew that Madhuri had not been away from it for any length of time—perhaps since Jai had brought her and installed her there.

I saw the bed where he must have died, but there were no signs of bloodstains on the Anatolian rug—nor any trace of the tragedy. The bed was as low as a charpoy —and I lifted the woven throw that covered it. That's what it was. A peasant's string bed. It must have been brought in—exchanged for the other one that matched the French gilt furniture, Louis XVI all the way. I opened the ornate wardrobe with its long beveled mirror, noticing my own paleness in the half light. One side held drawers with half moon cutouts for hand grips. I pulled them open one by one. They held saris of every color imaginable, sweaters, blouses, necklaces, bracelets, a small leather box, locked: probably more jewels. On the other side was the hanging closet. There was a long beige wool cape with heavy embroidery on the hem, and a mink cape. Her slippers were lined across the bottom of the wardrobe beside a wicker basket. Then my breath caught and held —I reached for a pair and carried them to the light to examine them. They were gold-embroidered brocade, tiny, with a small heel. And on one there was a small gold rosette. On the toe of the other, nothing except several raw-edged threads. So it was Madhuri who had been in Bill Holmes' suite the night he was murdered. I found it hard to swallow.

I walked back slowly, wondering what I should do— confront Madhuri? Park? No—There was nothing I could do. Just as I reached the wardrobe, a cobra dropped from the chest to the floor. I stopped, speechless—it must have been in the wicker basket! I watched as it slithered over the floor, long, lithe, silky yellow-brown, straight to the balcony. So this was where he stayed—well, he *was* a house pet! He crawled past me as though he knew where he was going and I had an absurd inclination to reach down and pet him. Imagine his making a home with Madhuri! But then she's probably used to cobras in houses. I followed him to the balcony.

Suddenly as I watched, amazed at my own casual acceptance of the reptile, the snake straightened up almost a third of its length and struck as a mongoose dashed from the fretted grill of the balcony. The rodent dodged the snake and lunged at him in a lightning jab. They struggled frantically, the snake writhing in every direction, his forked tongue darting, his fangs bright and white. I watched in horror, all my sympathy with the cobra. Then, just as suddenly as it had begun, it was over. The snake was dead, gripped tightly by the mongoose, twitching limply. My stomach turned, and I was conscious that my nails were cutting into the palms of my hands. I backed away from the balcony in the half-light of evening and stumbled back to the open door. I closed it, leaning against it weakly. Then, as my legs turned to water, I slid down to sit on the top step, with my head resting on my knees.

I don't know how long I was there. I didn't open my eyes or raise my head until I heard voices in Madhuri's apartment. It was dark. A darkness that was as tangible as a mist. I recognized Deleep Chatterjee's precise-dictioned voice saying in exasperated distress, "You have to know when he will be back—you have to know. Didn't he tell you?"

And Madhuri's whining reply, "But I tried—I tried to find out. I tell you I tried and tried. What else can I do? He hates me, I tell you—he tries to hide it, but he can't."

"I have to go to the Maharaja now. I'll come back later. Stay in your apartment until he returns."

"But that may not be for days!"

"Then stay for days. Don't you understand the importance of this?"

"After the others—you think I don't?"

"And after this you can go home to your father and tell him all has been accomplished."

There was a short pause and then I heard her scream and Deleep's quick footsteps as he hurried to her. *"Nulla Pambu*—he's dead—"

"You had no business keeping him here. I told you to get rid of him after the boy died—"

"I loved him—"

"Forget the snake, Madhuri. I command you to forget the snake."

I didn't hear her reply, but I heard the door slam behind Deleep. I didn't understand what I'd heard, but I knew it was important and I tried to sear the words into my brain so I wouldn't forget them. When I reached my room, I put the slippers in my suitcase. The heavy scent of gardenias rose from them and I was sick again.

To the tip of my toes I was sick. I retched and vomited and gagged until there was nothing in me, and still my stomach heaved and twisted and turned inside out, until I lay on the floor drenched in sweat, too weak to sit up. Finally I crawled to my bed and lay on it panting—taking deep breaths through my mouth like a dying fish, trying to control the muscles of my stomach. And I wondered again if someone was giving me a slow-acting poison—it was so strange that I'd been sick every day for a week.

Then suddenly a horrifying thought came to me. I counted mentally on my fingers— Dear God! Don't let it be! I was sick again, and I curled into a knot and wished I could die.

Elizabeth's baby came that night.

I was still awake, reliving every second of the nightmare that I knew had happened to me. What would I do? How could I—how could I have this baby! Then I heard Elizabeth call.

She was standing in the door gripping her body with both hands, her face twisted and frightened. "Bevan, I know you've been sick—I could hear you. I hate to bother you, but the baby—I'm sure he's on his way. I called Leela but she's gone. I can't understand." She gripped her stomach as a spasm of pain clutched her.

The strength that had deserted me flooded back and I jumped to my feet. "Leela! Leela!" I called. Onto the balcony I rushed. "Leela! Leela! Help—Elizabeth needs you—" But Leela didn't come. No one came. No one heard my call for help, no one. Leela, who had slept outside Elizabeth's door ever since she'd been at Khilar, had suddenly disappeared.

Elizabeth called and I hurried back to her. She was doubled over in a paroxysm of pain. I tried to remember everything I'd ever heard. A sheet to pull on? Hot water— for what? Time the pains—get my watch. Elizabeth—how long have you been having them? She could only shake her head, her face distorted in agony. I think you should walk—somewhere I've heard—

Oh, God—Elizabeth made a low moan that sounded like an animal cry and crumpled to the floor.

It lasted all night. Her screams tore me apart, and then when they became weaker it was worse. A pale green dawn dimmed the lamps before the baby came, in a spasm that ripped Elizabeth with one god-awful searing cry. The baby, a boy, burst into the room on the marble floor in a mixture of blood and water and gave a yelling squall. The cord—the cord had to be cut. Look—look frantically for something sharp—scissors—a knife—

I found the dagger in a table drawer and ripped some selvage off a sheet and knotted it around the cord. Then I took the dagger and separated the baby from its mother. I wrapped the baby in a towel and laid him on my bed.

I turned back to Elizabeth. She was dead.

And the Maharaja died that night.

chapter XI

Leela found us there, Elizabeth beneath the brocade cover-
let on the bathroom floor and me beside her, cuddling
her baby and crooning through cracked lips the only
lullaby I knew. *Bye-o baby bunting, Daddy's gone a-hunt-
ing, To get a tiger skin to wrap this baby bunting in,* over
and over—and over—unconscious of the words, unmindful
of their meaning, snuggling the baby in its towel blanket
close to me. He whimpered softly like a baby sparrow in
a nest. I couldn't whisper to him that his mother was
dead, that he had no one, no one at all to care—

I sat there heedless of the quick stir of people in the
apartment. I watched dully as they carried Elizabeth away.
But when they reached for the baby I sprang to my feet.
I snatched up the dagger I'd used to cut the cord that
bound Elizabeth's baby to her, and backed into a corner
in my bedroom and threatened anyone who came near.

It was Park who took him from me. His voice was
low and mesmerizing; his eyes clear and soft and sad.

"Bevan, the baby has to be bathed and fed. There is a nurse in the zenana waiting. Asha will protect him—believe me. He has to have proper care—"

And so I let him take the dagger and put it aside, and then, with infinite tenderness, he took the baby from me and handed him to Leela. She hurried through the swarm of servants, and then Park waved them away. My eyes burned and my arms were empty and I felt nothing at all at the nearness of Park. He told me then that the Maharaja had died. That was why Leela wasn't at Elizabeth's door. Everyone in the palace had been at the Raja's bedside. That was why no one heard my call.

He walked to the chest and picked up the dagger. "Do you know where you found this?"

I looked at it then—but the sight of it didn't shock me or make me feel anything.

It was the Deccan *Katar*. The same one that had killed Jai. The one that had killed Bill Holmes. And I didn't care. Without speaking, I walked to the table in Elizabeth's room and pulled out the drawer. He held the dagger in his hand, and I could see the blood dried on it.

I had to know. "Someone wants to kill the child—Park, is it you?"

He answered quietly, "No, Bevan. You may be sure of that."

"Elizabeth thinks so." *Elizabeth thinks—Elizabeth thinks—Elizabeth thinks.* The present tense again. Why do I keep thinking of the dead in the present tense?—Elizabeth and Bill—Bill, so long since I'd even thought of him. And the same Deccan *Katar* that had been used to kill him, I had used to separate the baby from Elizabeth.

Park laid the dagger on the desk and closed the drawer I'd opened. Then without turning around he said,

"I'm sorry I couldn't make things easier for Elizabeth. But God help me, Bevan, the boy will be protected. You can depend on it." Then he turned to me. There was something in his eyes I'd never seen before—but there was nothing in me to respond. He reached for my hand and asked me a surprising question. "Bevan, will you stay—will you stay here and help me care for him?"

I pulled my hand away quickly and looked at him. I knew all the suffering I'd felt that night was full upon my face. "Oh, no!" I cried. I turned away to the window, nervously fingering my throat, pushing my tangled hair away from my face. "Oh, no—*No!* I just want to leave. To leave as soon as I can."

His voice was low. "I understand. Elizabeth's funeral will be three days from now. Then the Maharaja's body will lie in state for a week. The astrologers are talking about an immediate investiture for the baby. I'd like you to stay for that. I'll make arrangements for you to leave immediately afterward."

I didn't answer. He turned and walked to the door. There was a pause before he said, "I'll send Leela to you." I heard the faint click of the latch as he closed it.

Turning from the window, I felt an immense loneliness, an ache of hollowness that translated itself to the image in the mirror of the gold and silver wardrobe. I stared at it. The reflection that stared back was gaunt, haggard with matted hair, deep circles and sunken cheeks. The sari I wore was stained with blood—and I didn't care. It was Elizabeth's blood—and Elizabeth was dead. What was it in the Bible? *Let the dead bury their dead.* So different from the *Gita—What is shall always be.*

Leela came then with a steaming bowl of broth and spooned it into me as if I were a baby. I remember vaguely that she bathed me and dressed me and put me to bed.

And through an eternity of darkness she lifted my head and fed me and put cool cloths on my forehead and combed my hair and crooned to me in Hindi much as I'd crooned to the baby. And once she brought him to me. The small baby and the old woman blurred together in a madonna image that made me smile. The dark wrinkled little woman in the white sari and the tiny brown baby with a mass of black hair standing on end, his fists doubled, his eyes squinting against the light—snuggled to her breast. She held him out for me to take and I shook my head. I knew that if ever I held him I'd never leave Khilar; that it would be an invisible chain I could not break. I was relieved when she took him out.

For three days I didn't leave my small quarters. Leela cared for me, babied me, fed and dressed me but no one came to inquire about me; no one seemed to care that I was still at the Khilar Palace. The day before the funeral I dressed and sat in the garden for awhile. But it was too lonely.

At high noon of the chosen day, Elizabeth was carried on her funeral bier to the burning ghat dressed in a red silk sari. Her body was covered with flowers, but next to her heart was a white rose I picked in the garden that morning. It—it seemed so American, that rose. I wanted it there. Leela dressed her hair and wove a veni, a crescent of yellow jasmine, to go across the heavy gold-brown bun.

Leela led me around the parapet of the roof of the palace where the other women were gathered. This time there was no tension. They greeted me with shadowed eyes as one of them. The Rani Asha drew me to her and said, "You are very brave."

But I wasn't brave enough to stay and watch as the flames ate Elizabeth's body and the smoke curled to the sky.

I went back to the apartment, walking aimlessly through it, touching the things she'd bought with Jai and had loved so much. I gathered her personal things and packed them. They'd go home with me. I stopped once and looked up the spiral stairs to Madhuri's apartment. I hadn't seen or heard of her since the night Elizabeth's baby was born. Neither had I seen Deleep Chatterjee. Then—suddenly—I remembered.

It had completely slipped my mind, in the trauma of Elizabeth and myself, that I had evidence connecting Madhuri to Bill's death. And in the conversation I heard between them—Madhuri and Deleep—more evidence that connected them with something else, and I didn't know just what. I knew though, that they were dangerous to the boy. And why that should be, I didn't understand.

Why had the Deccan *Katar* been in Elizabeth's room? Was it to throw suspicion on her? Was it even there to be at hand for someone to kill her? And possibly me? Such conjectures were foolish—but now I could talk to Park and warn him. I hesitated a minute, trying to synchronize my thoughts. If I knew the child was safe, I could leave Khilar Palace with my mind at ease. With no loose threads to unravel—*No loose threads?* Foolish woman! *You're carrying in your body the loosest thread of them all. What will you do when you get to America? With a bud of life growing within. You can't go back to your classes. What will you do?*

I went into the garden and walked its paths restlessly. Soft clouds drifted over the lake and I wondered if they were part of the spiraling smoke of Elizabeth's body. I felt a sickening sense of defeat—for myself and for her baby—a crawling nervous tension that gave me no rest. And I sent word by a servant that I needed to talk to His Highness, the Regent.

It was later when Park found me there. We walked silently for awhile; I knew he'd been at the burning ghat. As the senior member of the family it was his duty to light the flame and take the ashes. I knew too that now it was all over. Then we were on the dock by the launch where Elizabeth and I had walked the first day Park brought me to the palace. That day when I had expected to start home with Bill's body.

We sat on the bench that overlooked the small harbor, and he said, "I've talked to Corraway Sheridan—told him about Elizabeth, and why you stayed."

"And the baby?" I whispered.

"Yes. And that you'd be returning soon."

We were silent for several minutes, and then I said, "I'll mail you the Deccan *Katar* as soon as I get back."

He shook his head. "No, you mustn't do that. I—I'd rather you kept it." Again there was a long silence, then he added, "I told Sheridan I was withdrawing the injunction—that he could do anything he wanted with the collection."

I didn't answer. It seemed that time had telescoped and my perspective was all wrong; that I was looking through the big end, and everything that had any meaning was infinitesimal now. Only one thing was real and that was the life I carried—my past, my present, my future was all held in the cup of my hand. And I was frightened of it.

"I'm afraid for her child," I said.

"There's no need, Bevan. The boy will be secure. Not only is everyone in the palace committed to caring for him, but all of Kataipur—"

"I don't understand," I answered.

"Every Hindu in the Northeast and into the Himalayan regions knows, as surely as if he'd seen the magic passing, that the Maharaja's soul entered into the child's body just before he was born; that it was he who killed the American princess."

I think I gasped. The thought was so repugnant that I moved away from him on the bench and looked at him for the first time. "I—I think that's dreadful."

"No, on the contrary. I find it a very real, a healing thing—"

His face had a sadness that didn't carry the conviction of his words—but I didn't want to get into another argument with him about Hindu philosophy. I only said, "Elizabeth had an infinite capacity for suffering—I hope she's at peace now. No more lives—no more turning wheels."

"There are compensations in everything. Your own philosopher Emerson knew it. She had her unhappiness in this life; the next will be a better one."

"You really believe that, don't you?"

His eyes were partially shadowed, but the lake reflected in them and small speckles of amber glittered as he said, "I'm not the first—"

I wanted to cry, but my eyes were dry and hot and I stood up suddenly. "The night that—that Elizabeth's baby was born—I overheard Madhuri and Deleep Chatterjee talking. I didn't understand it, but I think they might be planning to harm the child. I also found a pair of her shoes and they matched a bow—a rosette—I found in Bill's room at the Moti Palace."

He nodded seriously. "Bevan, our police have been working very quietly, very efficiently, the Maharaja and I with them. We knew Elizabeth was in danger—she has been since Jai was killed. Bill's death was a surprise. Of course, we knew it wasn't suicide." He hesitated then and looked at me before he continued. "At first—at first I thought you'd had him get the *Katar* from Chatterjee. Then when you were in the office, I knew—I knew that you'd had nothing to do with it. Will you forgive me?"

I didn't answer. I kept my eyes riveted across the lake watching the play of light on the ripples. What was he trying to tell me?

"Suddenly Bill was in his way," he added.

"In whose way?" I asked.

"Chatterjee's. He's in prison in Darampur. He implicated Madhuri and now they're blaming each other." He paused. Neither of us spoke for several minutes. I don't think I was surprised. After a while he began again. "Madhuri was sent here by her father, who was Jai's father-in-law. It was revenge, you see. Jai was married to a young Rajasthan princess, Gayatri. A beautiful girl. But it wasn't a successful match. The Raja had planned to send her back with her dowry. But she took sick and died. Asha thinks it was peritonitis from a burst appendix—no one knows. Certainly she wasn't poisoned as her father intimated. This happened while I was in London. She was cremated at the family ghat. And having died a member of the family—that was that so far as the Raja was concerned. He didn't return her dowry. Then Jai and Elizabeth were married. Jai didn't know that Madhuri was Gayatri's older, widowed sister—and that she'd been sent to kill all the Raja's heirs. She almost succeeded."

"But I thought—" I almost choked on the words, "that she and you—killed Bill—I heard you threaten him at Sheridan's."

"Did you? I may have felt like it at the time, but it's not the way I'd choose to get rid of leeches like Holmes." He pulled out a package of cigarettes and offered me one. I shook my head. He picked one carefully as though it was the most important thing in the world, and lighted it. The smoke that spiraled up from it made me tense my jaws to keep from crying out. I think he saw—because he flipped the cigarette into the lake and began talking.

"It was Deleep Chatterjee who was responsible for Holmes' death. Chatterjee recognized Madhuri when Jai brought her to Khilar. He'd been at her father's when he'd arranged for Jai's marriage. He guessed why Madhuri was here and it fit into his plans. He'd been selling state treasures—that is, temple sculptures and various things from the palace—for years to Corraway Sheridan, and Jai had asked him about it."

He paused a minute, picked up a pebble, and tossed it into the lake, and we sat there watching the ripples it made. Then he commenced again. "To be honest, this traffic in antiquities has been going on for years. It wasn't something Deleep thought up. The Raja had done it when he was the Yuvraj and needed extra funds. He stopped when he became Maharaja. But Deleep kept it up. This time when Bill came to pick up the Shiva and Parvati statue, Deleep tried to cut himself in on the deal. The priest wanted to back out after the child was killed, and Deleep was blackmailing them both. I don't know for sure—no one will—but Bill must have threatened Deleep, because Deleep forced Madhuri to kill him. She came to Kataipur the day of my birthday, ostensibly to help me celebrate, but really just for one thing—to kill Bill. She had the Deccan *Katar*. Deleep had gotten it for her to kill Jai."

"I have to know—" I interrupted slowly, "how did Elizabeth come to be in Madhuri's apartment?"

"Deleep, besides being the Raja Hari's secretary, was his doctor—not a physician in the Western sense, but he understood hypnosis and had a vast knowledge of herbs and medicines. I really don't think he abused those gifts until he knew Jai had found out about the smuggling. It was very easy to hypnotize Elizabeth and make her think she'd killed her husband."

I sighed. I felt an indescribable tiredness. There was much I'd like to know, but I was too weary to ask questions.

Then Park continued, "The Raja knew what was going on, but he was too feeble to gather the proof himself. That's why he sent for me. That's why he wanted you with Elizabeth every minute. He knew she would be the next."

We were silent for a while and then he said, "The investiture of the child will be in ten days. Ordinarily, it wouldn't be so soon, but the astrologers think it's the proper time. It's just as well."

I had started to speak when I saw the snake. It came from the big fountain where Elizabeth and I had seen it so often, the sun shining on its sleek brown-gold back. It rose slowly in front of us, and I gripped Park's arm. He looked at me in surprise. "What's the matter? The snake, Naja, has always been here—"

"But you don't understand," I shouted at him, staring at the snake, hypnotized. "I saw him killed on Madhuri's balcony—a mongoose—"

"That was a different one. Deleep told us Madhuri brought it from her home to kill Krishna or Jai—or Elizabeth. The dead snake was still in Madhuri's apartment when she was arrested."

Things were fitting into place like pieces of a jigsaw puzzle. Everything dovetailed neatly. Everything except Elizabeth—and me. We were the round pegs in the square holes. She hadn't conformed, and it had killed her. I couldn't adapt, so I was going home a misfit—an alien in two worlds. Now the man I loved was beside me, and somehow it didn't matter. I was emotionally drained, lacking all capacity to feel. It was so long since I'd cried. Not since that day at Shiva's Temple on the island when I'd wept and Elizabeth had taken me into her arms and comforted me. She didn't know that it was because of Park I cried.

One more question. "What will they do to the Kali priest who killed his little grandson?"

"He was brought here and tried. He and his son have both been committed to an asylum."

I didn't say anything. Then he reached for my hand and held it—until I pulled it away. "Good-bye, Bevan."

"Good-bye." Our eyes caught and held briefly. I looked away first. I heard the sound of his steps leaving until they grew faint and disappeared. All I could hear then was a garden full of sound. Birds and a cicada, wild geese over the lake, the doves that nested in the trumpet vine, the fountain splashing in its basin.

A glorious iridescent blue butterfly lighted on a red hibiscus blossom and regarded me gravely. I reached out and it moved to my finger with the gentleness of an angel's breath, and I almost called it Elizabeth. *God!* I thought, *I'm losing my mind*—I shook it off as though it had stung me. And I hurried inside.

Somehow the week passed. I didn't see Park again. The Maharaja Hari Pita-Singh Vehta was lying in state in the throne room and there was much activity. Leela told me that dignitaries from all over India had come to pay their respects, government officials from Delhi, and countless representatives from former ruling families of the now nonexistent princely kingdoms. They all came.

Then there was the funeral. I joined the women of the zenana at the parapet of the roof. We watched the thin spiral of smoke waft up from the bank of Lake Kalpa. There were tears from the women and soft murmuring. I heard an occasional Sanskrit chant and the Rani Asha quoted from the *Bhagavad-Gita:* the Lord Krishna saying, *I have passed through many births, And so have you, Arjuna. But I remember all of these. Enemy of the foe, you do not remember.* Then she pulled the pallav of her sari over her face, bowed her head, and walked to the stairs. The others, even the little girls, followed, doing as she did, and I felt no strangeness when I did the same.

The investiture of the infant, now officially named Bharata Man Pita-Singh Vehta, took place at noon two days later in the audience hall of Khilar Palace. I stood with the women of the zenana on the balcony and watched from behind the marble screen as Park, wearing white achkan and chridars and a white turban with a white cockade, his ribbon of office as regent, a garland of jasmine, and his sword in a white scabbard, entered behind the royal priest. Another priest carried the baby draped in yards of white brocade. His small brown head bobbed as the priest walked with him, unaccustomed to carrying such a wee infant. Other priests lined the way to the throne, and the hall was filled with dignitaries and local chieftains. Everyone was dressed in white—mourning the old Maharaja.

I watched the ceremony as the priests chanted and read from the holy books and prayed for the long life of the infant Maharaja. Then the child was handed to Park, who held him as the royal priest put the sacred vermillion paste on the baby's forehead. With this act, he proclaimed him Maharaja of Kataipur, the forty-fifth in a long line of rulers which claimed its descent from the sun through Lava, son of Rama.

At the same time I heard the guns of Valhargath Fort

boom out a nineteen-salvo salute. A contingent of the Kataipur Armed Constabulary presented a guard of honor while the state anthem was played. And the flags on the palace went up to full mast to the accompaniment of shehnai music.

Immediately afterward, the local chieftains (the *sirdars* and *jagirdars*) pledged their allegiance to the baby ruler as though Indira Gandhi's recent edict had never been made. Led by the official dignitaries of the city of Kataipur, they walked up to the baby, held now by an aide, and offered him gold sovereigns, silver coins, and paper currency. Park accepted the offerings gracefully on behalf of the child and threw them onto a piece of gold-embroidered velvet held by two courtiers.

Then Park took the child and walked the length of the audience hall, coming to the zenana balcony where we had watched the proceedings. He bowed, touching the feet of the Rani Asha, asked her blessing on the baby, and then turned to the mother of Jai, the grandmother of the child, and asked her blessing also. The women had tears in their eyes as they gave it, and my own were misty. As he rose he looked at me a long time without speaking, and the small baby opened his eyes and looked at me, too. Then he gave a sharp bellow and turned red in the face. Park said, "Leela—he is a splendid Maharaja, now give him his lunch." He left the baby with her, bowed again to the Maharani, and left the balcony. I knew that Elizabeth's baby would be safe in his care. And I went back to Elizabeth's apartment to pack.

I pulled my suitcase from the closet, and as soon as I opened it I found the brown paper package from the Kali shrine still folded in plastic. It was the first time I'd thought of it since I'd wrapped it up at the Moti Palace. And still I couldn't throw the damn thing away—I shoved it back in a corner and covered it with sweaters and under-wear, trying to hide it in a deep corner of my memory as well. I laid out a suit to wear, and a blouse and shoes. The Western clothes looked strange and the fabric felt unfamiliar.

That night there were fireworks over the fort. I watched with the women of the zenana from the roof of the palace. The sprays of fire reflected in the lake like clusters of stars falling to meet themselves, and before they could disappear on its black surface, great new clusters in red and gold and green and blue burst in the sky to illuminate the hills and the lake and all the palace and reflect in the faces of the women and the little girls. In the court-yard and in the compound were thousands of small earthenware cups filled with lighted wicks in mustard oil like so many fallen stars. Strings of lights festooned the trees, and as suddenly as it had begun, it was over. Gradually the women left the roof, until there were only the Rani Asha and me. It was cold, and one by one the lights went out. A night bird called.

"I'll not see you tomorrow—" the Rani said slowly.

"No, Highness. I'd rather not say good-bye—"

"You know the law of karma, Bevan. Yesterday is linked with today as is tomorrow, a circle unending."

I bowed my head and nodded. I couldn't speak. She added, "A breath, a whisper, and life begins again. Life renews itself at each great happening— So there is no need for good-byes. Give me your hand, Bevan. A bit of my heart is there."

I knelt in front of her and kissed her hand. She stooped and put her arms around me and touched her cheek to mine. "Another day—"

I was ready early the next morning. Leela was asleep at the door, and I slipped by her and went into the garden.

A cold mist had gathered over the lake, and soft gray tendrils of it reached into the garden. The morning glories and the hibiscus were still closed in tight trumpets. But there was a freshness over it all. Roses drooped from a heavy dew. The birds were busy; they chattered and fussed and fluttered through the trees. I remembered the first time I'd seen the garden, when it had seemed a haven of evil and death. I smiled, remembering how my imagination had made so much of a mosquito spray. Now the garden was coming alive—but I'd not be here to see its full birth.

I felt his approach before I saw him. A strange extrasensory perception made me know when he was near—as a piece of metal feels the pull of a magnet. I didn't turn around.

"The car is here. I sent a bearer for your things. Will you have breakfast?"

"No—nothing, thank you."

"Then a cup of coffee?"

"No, no." I was suddenly frantic to leave. "I must go now, please." So he followed me to the door, and there was the servant with the crest on his turban and the yellow sash, and he opened the tall doors. It was the first time I'd been outside the palace since I'd come that day after Bill's death—so long ago. I took a deep breath and, with every bit of intestinal fortitude that I'd inherited from midwestern pioneers, I braced my shoulders, looked Prakash in the eyes, and smiled a great, genial, touristy smile, and said, "Goodbye—if you're ever in the States—" and I couldn't finish. Dear God, no! He was the last person I'd want to see in the States.

He stooped over my hand and almost kissed it, but didn't. He had a faint smile on his face when he said, "Good-bye, Dr. Bevan Blakley. Khilar Palace will never be quite the same—" He saw me to the car and closed the door, then motioned the driver to leave.

As we turned from the palace drive, I saw the old sadhu sitting beneath the peepul tree in the courtyard. I reached over to tap the driver on the shoulder and said in Hindi, "Stop—stop for a minute—" I climbed out of the car quickly and ran to him. I made a deep obeisance, reached into my purse, and dropped some rupee notes into his begging bowl. "I'm leaving, *Panditji,* give me your blessing—for several months more—"

"I know, daughter." He raised his hand and closed his eyes. "The track of Vishnu's wheel," he said slowly, "is rock-filled and abounds with fear for the faint. Be serene, daughter, the temple bells will ring for you and the child."

I bit my lip. How in the name of God could he know? Or was it Elizabeth's child he meant? I looked back at the palace. Park was still standing there. The tall carved doors were open behind him, and the doorman in his white turban with the bright cockade and the royal crest was beside him. The two soldiers stood at attention on either side. I glanced away quickly and climbed into the car. It was hard—somehow my roots had gone down awfully deep in a very short time.

The soldiers at the gate saluted as we passed.

chapter XII

I stood on the bank of University Lake watching the small bonfire blazing between three carbon-smudged stones. The smoke followed me restlessly; the fire snapped and bristled, burning the package that contained the sacred and smelly residue from the Kali Shrine in Kataipur.

My eyes smarted, and tears that had been dry for so long were nervously close to the surface. Suddenly the strength that had sustained me through Elizabeth's labor, and her cremation, the investiture of the baby, the long trip back, the heartbreaking task of telling Miss Edith, deserted me. An involuntary gasp broke from my throat and I dropped to my knees, burying my face in my hands. And for long minutes I let my agony escape in great racking sobs.

It had been a short time—but not really. An eternity that covered birth and death and conception and future births and deaths— Oh, Kipling knew all right. There is no blending of the East and West. There is no way they can become an homogenized whole. I knew. God only knows how well I knew. I'd circled the world and was back now where I'd started from. Back home to lick my wounds, to wonder if there is any way a life that has been ripped apart can heal itself.

I took a lung-filling breath of the cold air and stood up. I wiped my eyes, and blew my nose, and straightened my shoulders. Only last week I'd felt the touch of life inside. I'd tried to tell Uncle Coe—and I couldn't. I'd tried to tell Lane when I'd asked for a leave of absence—and I couldn't. There was no way I could go to them and say, *I'm going to have a baby—yes, of course I know who the father is, but he doesn't want to marry—not me. He'll marry some dark-eyed northern princess dressed in brocade and they'll take the traditional three steps together, and she'll bear him children, and they'll grow up in Khilar Palace with the small Maharaja. They'll play in the garden with the tame cobra, and never be afraid—they'll fish the banks of Kalpa Lake, and visit the Shiva temple and ring the bells at the Kali Shrine. They'll watch fireworks over Valhargath Fort at Dussehra, they'll light small candles in earthenware saucers at Diwali, and splash each other with colored water at the Holi Festival of spring. And they'll never know they have a small half brother or sister living in the States—a bastard child without a father.*

The flame had died and there was only smoke. It had ceased its fitful trailing, and in the quiet morning beside the lake it was spiraling straight up, up in a thin transparent plume that wavered neither to the right nor to the left. Straight up like the smoke from the funeral ghat beside the Kalpa. Straight up like the smoke from the shrine when Elizabeth's flower was laid on the flame. Straight up to a foreign goddess, Kali, returning to her the rice cake, the marigold, the ribbons that she had blessed in her butcher shrine beside a mountain stream and given back to me. The rancid ghee that loaded the rice cake sputtered in the heat and sounded alive. I shivered and knew that it was more than the bitter cold of the early winter morning that sent chill bumps across my back.

I had driven along the rutted track and parked my car in the same place I'd left it months earlier. The lake hadn't changed, nor had the lovers' lane that meandered around it; not even the thin finger of land that branched out from the frozen marsh beyond the grove of blackjack oaks, winter-naked now except for a scattering of curled-up leaves. I left the car in the lane and carried my package through ankle-deep leaves and dead grass to the graveled bank, pockmarked with past picnic fires. I remembered well enough when I'd been here before, and the bitterness I felt at going to India for Miss Dameron. I remembered the curiosity I had about Park's interest in the Deccan *Katar*. How I'd taken it from its case in the museum and had sat here on this stone and held it in my hands. So long ago—three lifetimes, Elizabeth's, Bill's and mine. No, five. Elizabeth's baby and my own. The small brown bag, greasy and rancid, had come with me to Khilar and then on the long trip home. I couldn't carry it with me always, so I'd brought it to the lake.

The bank was thick with stones, and close by the water's edge I built a tiny altar. It was a triangular affair which I knew Kali would understand. I laced it with small brush and leaves and wove a frame of blackjack twigs across the top, and on that I placed this once-blessed offering, the little package wrapped in the brown paper that had been the liner for a wastebasket in the hotel, and that had traveled with me halfway round the world. I flamed my lighter and held it to the brush.

It caught and sizzled and blazed—and the smell of it

was exactly that of the mother temple in Kataipur where blood sacrifices were the norm. Every Tuesday and Saturday the saturnalia of bloodletting. Rain or shine, monsoon or drouth, bring your goats or sheep or chickens, or in the darkness of the night bring a child—but not a cow. Oh, God, no! Not a cow—

It burned slowly as though the goddess Kali was reluctant to accept what she had previously given. The stones turned black, as black as the face of the goddess. Slowly, fitfully, the package burned and drifted in transparent wisps to blend with the sky.

The morning was cold and still, the air icy and damp with a hint of snow. My breath hung in a rimed vapor that was gray like everything around me. Scattered groves of trees were misty skeletons accented here and there with transplanted gray-black conifers. The weeds, the grasses, the wild berry-bearing shrubs, the cattails in the marsh that had somehow escaped the dried bouquet enthusiasts —all were dead. Across the lake, on beyond the rise of Academy Hill, the spire of Old Central was faintly etched in the gray sky. Everything was the same—all shades of gray. The sky, the lake, the hill, the smoke. There was no breeze to ripple the water, and it was like opaque glass.

Then, drawing strength from the blaze, the smoke swirled in evil circles, and the smell reminded me of those things I would remember as long as I lived. And I wondered if that was to be Kali's curse—or the sadhu's blessing —that I could never forget.

I glanced around, unconsciously furtive. I was alone. There were no early-morning winter fishermen; no budding geologists hunting specimens; and plainly, no lovers. Only me. Me—and a black-souled Hindu goddess who demanded blood sacrifices and rejected the withered marigold Elizabeth had sent her. How would she feel about my own marigold, and the withered mala and the dried rice cake and the red and yellow ribbons?

There was a peacefulness about the winter day that belied the churning of my heart, and about this university city where I'd been born and reared, where I'd awakened to emotional puberty, where I'd returned seeking sanctuary—where I found no peace. The fire was dying.

Faint scraggy fingers of smoke poked up from the ashes, but I couldn't leave. There was something more to be done. I pulled my handkerchief from my pocket. It was still damp from tears and, as I stretched it on the ground close beside my fire, bits of sooty ashes drifted to it and stuck. The rice cake was a brittle piece of charcoal and I crumbled it with a stone. Then I scraped the ashes from my offering onto the linen square and folded it to make a pouch.

My boots crunched on the frozen ground as I crossed to the tip of the peninsula. I waited only a second before I flung the small linen sack as far as I could into the lake. I watched the handkerchief flutter open and then watched as it sank, leaving dark specks of ashes and charcoaled rice cake floating on the surface. They made interlocking ripples that grew and grew until they met the tip of the land where I stood.

I turned then and without a backward glance walked to my car. Everything was finished. Nothing bound me to India now. Well—only a baby whose feathery movement against my heart was fairly regular now—

The drive back to the apartment was an automatic thing. It had begun to snow, great wet flakes the size of quarters that splashed against my windshield and drifted ahead of me in every direction. It was a heavy gray day.

At the apartment, I slowed but didn't stop. Suddenly

I had to be with someone. I turned the car around and headed for the old Sheridan mansion. I'd seen Uncle Coe several times since I'd come back. But I didn't go over there with the lighthearted feeling of belonging I'd always felt before. Now I tensed when he looked at me. I could remember his saying, "You've got to level with me, girl. If it happens—tell me." I could see him sometimes looking at me curiously—and so I'd space my visits farther and farther apart. And when Bertha would call and ask me to dinner, I'd make excuses. When Christmas came I'd gone to the Coast—without telling anyone where to find me. And afterward, I'd torn into the restoration work that was waiting for me, applied myself to recataloging the items in the museum, and generally kept busy at contrived work. Anything to keep my mind off—off the future. And if anyone noticed my thickening waistline, they were tactful enough not to mention it. Although, truthfully, I dressed to hide it. But the time would come—was practically here—and I had to do something. The time had come to talk to Uncle Coe.

I parked in front of the iron gates and walked up the brick path. The leaves had mostly blown away or were soggy damp with snow. The flakes hit me in the face, clung to my eyelashes. They had begun to stick to the brick walk and frost the dried grass. At the top of the steps I stomped my boots and then brushed them on the tufted carpet at the entry. I pushed open the door and called, "Uncle Coe!" And he answered, "Bevan—come in!"

He was in the library, getting to his feet from his easy chair as I entered. A log fire crackled in the fireplace, and he hugged me to him. "Take off your coat. Damn, but I've missed you. How can you stay so busy?"

"Believe me, it's not easy." I looked at him directly

and seriously. "It's awfuly hard to stay as busy as I need to —to try to forget when the thing you're trying to forget is growing larger—and larger—"

He eyed me for a minute and then picked up his pipe from the tray beside him and filled it from the humidor. "I think it's time we talked, Bevan."

I avoided his glance and looked in the fire. If I cried I'd kill myself. "It's happened, Uncle Coe—just as you said. You've won the Emerald Kali and the Deccan *Katar*. Except I hope you'll send them—the *Katar* and the Kali— back to India."

"If that's what you want." He studiously avoided looking at me, busy lighting his pipe.

I ran my tongue over my lips. It was harder even than I'd expected. I took a heavy back-hunching breath and blurted out, "I'm pregnant—"

"Do you want to tell me about it?"

I shook my head. There was no way I could tell this man I'd loved since I was a child that I was pregnant by his bastard son—that I was going to bear his grandchild. Then he said a surprising thing. "I'd like to adopt the child, Bevan. You can take your sabbatical early, and go anywhere you'd like. I'll join you later, and we'll have your baby. And he—she—will be surnamed Sheridan."

I started crying then. And laughing too. Suddenly there was no problem. Why hadn't I come to him earlier? He made no move to comfort me, except to hand me a handkerchief. I couldn't seem to find mine—I'd forgotten it was at the bottom of University Lake. I blew my nose, but the tears kept seeping. And then Uncle Coe said, "Bevan, I'm going to tell you a story. A true story, and it's a love story. It might help you—it might not. But stick your feet up to the fire and don't say anything until I'm finished."

So I propped my feet up on the stool, lighted a cigarette, and waited for him to tell me his story. For all I knew, he would make something up to take my mind off my problem. He'd done it before.

"It was during World War II," he began, " and I had been recalled from Delhi. My reserve commission was activated, and I was sent to London as a member of the American military mission to observe the results of the Luftwaffe attacks. It was during the worst of the bombings —what Churchill called England's finest hour. And at the Foreign Ministry I met the Yuvraj of Kataipur. He had just married his third wife, a much younger woman, and was on some mission for his father. He was probably fifty-five or so. She was a princess from a southern Indian state and spoke not only several languages, French and German and English, fluently, but Hindi and a strange dialect called Telugu.

"At a gathering one evening someone in Intelligence found out she spoke Telugu and asked the Yuvraj if he'd have any objections to having her do some codes in the language. They were sending an agent, who had grown up in Southern India and who also spoke the language, into occupied France, and she could be a great help.

"Well, when appealed to in that sense, there wasn't much he could do about it. I met them at a dinner one night, and since we had many mutual friends in Delhi we got along fine. And his wife—she was the loveliest woman I'd ever seen. There's no way to describe how I felt when I met her. I think we both knew almost before introductions were completed. She had brown eyes and brown hair doubled up in a bun at her neck, and there were seed pearls woven through it. She was wearing a pale yellow sari and emeralds in her ears. Her hands were small and her fingers long, and every movement they made was graceful. Her smile was something from heaven, and I've never ceased loving her from that day to this."

I knew what he was going to say. I knew he'd fallen in love with the Rani Asha, and he was telling me about it. And sooner or later he would get to Park. That would be my cue to tell him that Park was the father of my child. But I'd not do it. That secret would go to the grave with me.

"Then the Maharaja died, and Yuvraj Hari had to return to India. But the work Asha was doing was so important that he was prevailed upon to let her stay in London until the agent could complete his job—it would only be a month. Then she was to rejoin her husband in Kataipur as the Maharani.

"Well, there was no way I could stay away from her. We were together constantly. Then the agent returned and she went back to India. I was able to pull some strings, and got transferred back to Delhi. Anywhere, I thought, as long as it's India and I can be closer to her. What I didn't know was that she left England pregnant with my child—

"The Maharaja sent word to me in Delhi—to come to the palace on a certain night at midnight. When I got there I was surprised to see him enter with a servant woman following dressed to leave. She was carrying a baby—a brand-new baby. There was a lot of pale fuzz on its head and its skin was translucent and clear. I think I aged a hundred years in that minute. He told me the woman was Leela, who would nurse the baby—that the baby was born at the Shiva Temple in the lake—and for me to take the child and never come back. And I—I never went back. Not back to Kataipur.

"I was engaged to a fine young woman in my home town, and I started to bring the baby back to her, thinking we'd marry and give it a home. But I couldn't. I knew I could never love or live with anyone else."

I wondered when his rambling narrative would end. I glanced at him, at his shaggy brows over eyes pale with age, and his gaze met mine clear and direct. "I had a friend here, an M.D. He was some years older than I and had a son and daughter-in-law—childless. I suggested that they adopt this baby, and they did."

Suddenly I felt squeamish and I couldn't understand why. Chill bumps pricked my skin and my breath was short and shallow. "His son and daughter-in-law were killed in a plane crash, and my friend raised my baby. He was a prominent doctor here, Dr. Allan Blakley."

I sat there for a full minute or more while his words sank in. Then I moved out of the chair without really thinking about it, and fell beside him and buried my face in his lap. I wept then. I wept, and he knelt beside me and held me and wept with me.

Long afterward I sat on the stool beside his chair, and we held hands and talked. We would never get enough of talking. "I saw the Rani Asha—" I told him. And everything that had happened between us I remembered and told him. Even the silent confrontation with the Maharaja. And he told me how Leela brought the Emerald Kali with her wrapped in the infant's things in the valise, and how I learned Hindi before I learned English. And how, when I was two years old, he had sent Leela back to Asha.

It was easy enough then to tell him about Park. And how I'd thought Park was his son—because gossip never truly dies in a small town or a small country.

"Park was a younger brother of the Maharaja. His mother died when he was born, and the Raja raised him. But gossip will root anywhere—particularly as the Rani Asha had a child, secretly—"

We were silent for a long time, sitting there holding

hands. The firelight flickered on his face, his white hair, his strong hands. *And all the time the Rani had known!* When she'd sent me the saris and the slippers. When she'd asked about Uncle Coe. And the Raja—had he wanted to see us together, mother and child? Uncle Coe —could I ever call him Father?—brought me back to the present by squeezing my hand.

"Well, I didn't expect it to be Prakash," he said. "He's the last one—and I didn't expect it to happen so soon. But I wanted you to know the absolute ecstasy of love—and the absolute depths of losing it. Only then have you lived. Your life is a tapestry woven of rich threads on a somber warp—you'll have as many happy memories in the future as you've had anguished ones in the past."

"The woman, Uncle Coe, the woman you were engaged to—it was—"

He nodded. "Yes. Edith Dameron. As fine a woman as God ever put on this earth. But I didn't love her enough. So she didn't marry, and I didn't—and we've each had our separate hell. The dark side of the coin."

I stood up and straightened my shoulders. And when I looked down at him I smiled. "I know where I want my baby born."

"And where is that, Bevan?"

"In India. I don't care where. On either coast—to the north or south, but I want him to have an Indian ayah, to grow up speaking Hindi, to know what it is—this mysticism that enfolds the Hindu. My roots are reaching back, deep into a world I don't quite understand. But I'm going to try to make it mine. And I'm going back to Kataipur—someday—"